Liz

TREEHUGGER

Trees are love

By
Shamus Flaherty

authorHOUSE®

AuthorHouse™
1663 Liberty Drive
Bloomington, IN 47403
www.authorhouse.com
Phone: 1-800-839-8640

First published by AuthorHouse 1/8/2010

ISBN: 978-1-4490-3194-7 (sc)

Printed in the United States of America
Bloomington, Indiana

This book is printed on acid-free paper.

Author's Note

This novel is a work of fiction based on the real life heroics of Matt Largess.

CHAPTER 1

The first time I ever met Matt Largess was at a meeting of the Jamestown Tree Committee in the middle of winter inside the old Town Hall. I was working as a reporter for The Jamestown Press and was sent out to cover the meeting. I'd done it a couple times before and it wasn't so bad; that is to say it was pretty boring but not half as bad as sitting in on the Zoning Board or Harbor Commission meetings, which ran about twice as late as the tree thing.

So I walked in there and there was Matt sitting down at one end of the old wooden cafeteria-style table with a few of the other tree-folk. I had never seen him before. He was absent the first two meetings I covered. I know that for a fact because I distinctly remember writing down "Matt Largess—absent." Besides that, I'd been warned about him by the old guy who ran the meetings. He mentioned something about how things went much smoother without him and said, "Wait 'til you meet him… you'll see," and rolled his eyes.

I knew it had to be him when I first made eye contact with him. He had a familiar insane spark behind his pale blue eyes, something I recognized from a friend's battle with manic depression, and he spoke to me without a second's hesitation.

"Hey! What's up, man? A young guy. Yeah! You need a seat. Here, come sit down," he said. He pulled out an aluminum folding chair next to him and patted the seat with his palm. He had a stocky body like a 50-gallon drum, a shiny bald head with close shaved tufts of whitish-gray hair over his ears, and those crazy blue eyes with the mini fireworks show going on. His skin was weathered brown from a lifetime of working out in the sun. He was dressed in chaps, even though it was 7 at night in the middle of winter. And the chaps were clean as can be, as if he considered them evening-wear.

Now, you have to realize how quiet these meetings usually were. The first couple times I went, I made the mistake of showing up a few minutes early. It was awful. I said hello to the five or six people who were there and otherwise kept my mouth shut. They weren't much for small talk. Every time someone cleared his throat, every time a chair skidded on the worn linoleum, every time a paper crumbled it was like a bullhorn blast to the face, blowing your hair back from the force of it. It was a small open room in the common area of the town hall, surrounded by bookshelves and file cabinets.

Now here was this guy. This backwoods chain saw maniac with the chaps on.

"Sure," I said, laughing at him. I went over and took a seat and introduced myself.

"Hey, Shamus. Matt Largess. What are you doing here? I mean, where'd you come from? You're not a Jamestown kid, are you?"

At this point, one of the other tree guys decided to come to my rescue. "Jesus, Matt. Will you take it easy on the kid? You're gonna scare him right out of here. He works for the Press. Leave him alone."

"No. It's fine. I don't care," I said, although I was grateful for the interruption. I didn't come out to make any new friends. I came here to get the info, which was all completely useless to me, and write my story so I could get my sixty bucks and with any luck get home for the fourth quarter of the Celtics game. It was a little weird how this guy had taken so much of an interest in me so quickly. It may not sound like much but it was not normal, how excited he seemed.

And he kept at it. I could see that he basically wanted my whole life story, so after his first couple questions I gave him the abridged version of my life. I told him: I'm twenty-six. I'm not a Jamestown kid. I grew up in Warwick. I work part time for the Press right now. My wife and I just moved here from Martha's Vineyard. I was a landscaper there, and I'm looking to start up my own business here once the weather breaks. I enjoy writing, music, drinking, and long walks on the beach.

Now, your average person might get a little self-conscious after a remark like that. One might think, *Oh. Was I too forward? Is this kid busting my balls, or is he just playing around?*

Not Matt. "Yeah!" he roared. "Awesome. You're gonna start a business around here? That's great. It's a good spot. I grew up here. I've had my tree business here for twenty-seven years. You'll do great. Make enough to raise a family… all that. I could probably help get you started for your business. *Hey!* Do you need a job right now? Tomorrow? I could give you some work until you get started on your own. Might take a while. First year'll be slow. I---"

"All right," chimed in the old moderator of the meeting; a tall cotton-topped gentleman in a red flannel shirt with thick reading glasses. He peered over the rims of the lenses as he addressed the gathering. "Let's get this meeting started," he announced, clearing his throat. The other committee members shuffled through their packet of papers. Matt had nothing. He held his hands folded out in front of him on the bare dark-stained plywood of the table.

"Are you serious about the work?" I asked him, in a low voice so the meeting could begin.

"Yeah. I need you," he responded.

He *needed* me? I just met the guy two minutes ago and he already *needed* me. That was big. I would have felt better if he said something like, "Sure, I could use the help." But *need?*

"What do you need?" I asked. "A guy to drag brush and run it through the chipp-ah?" I asked, laying down my best Rhode Island accent, which at one point in my college days I made a conscious effort to get rid of.

"More or less. Come on. Do you want the job or not? Let's go."

I considered my options for a moment before responding. They weren't many. I was making two hundred bucks a week from the paper. I'd been in town for two weeks and had nothing else lined up. Rent was $1200 and was due in two more weeks.

"Absolutely," I said. "Can I start tomorrow?"

"Yeah! All right!" Matt answered, loud enough to make the moderator stop what he was saying and cast a glare of reproach.

"Sorry about that," I said, apologizing for both of us.

The guy just continued staring at Matt and shook his head. Then, when he continued on with the meeting, Matt went right on talking. And I mean *on*. It didn't stop for basically the whole meeting. He'd go at it for about five minutes strong and then take a break, and I'd think: *Wow. Thank God. That could be the end of it*. But after the first couple pauses I realized this was just a pattern in a never-ending cycle.

The fact that he was whispering didn't help much. It wasn't like the place was an auditorium. When there's six people in a small room and one of them's whispering while the others are trying to talk, it's pretty noticeable. If this was school, he would have been sent to the principal's office. It put me in a tough situation. Not that I really cared about it that much, but this was a job for me. I was supposed to be doing my job of sitting there, keeping my mouth shut and writing down what everyone else said, not undermining the whole meeting by whispering back and forth with this lunatic.

I started to get worried about losing my job with the paper. After all, I was new. It's easy to fire a new guy. You just put him out before he really gets in. So I tried to give

Matt only one-word responses without really looking at him to show him I was done. It didn't phase him. I even resorted to completely ignoring him. Nothing. He went right on talking.

He went on and on about his "operation." I gathered after some time that this was how he referred to his tree business. He told me how he loves trees, how he talks to trees, how he wants to save trees, basically how he wants to make love to trees. (He didn't actually say he wanted to make love to trees, but that's how I described it to my wife later that night.) He told me about all of his trucks, described the two or three guys that worked for him in detail... what they looked like, how they worked, what their outside interests were... everything. He described his chipper down to the model number. He asked me if I was going to plant all native plant material once I had my own business. He recommended that I should. He asked me about my writing. He was confused and thought for some reason that I was some kind of prize-winning journalist. I didn't tell him that—he kind of made it up himself while I ignored him or nodded my head "yes" or "no." He informed me in a voice that was not nearly discreet enough for the circumstances that, "These people are all blow-hards. Not Dave. I like Dave. They all talk and never get shit done."

I had to hide my grin in my notebook after he said that, and that just fired him up even more.

The weird thing was that by the end of it, I liked the guy. There was a point at the beginning of his ranting where I definitely decided to back out of the job with him.

I figured he was some kind of weirdo and I couldn't tolerate it. But by the end of it, I was willing to give it a shot. At least he was a weirdo who *knew* he was a weirdo. He could laugh at himself and wanted you to laugh with him. And he seemed like a nice enough, generous guy. He was willing to give me some work when I didn't have any. That was enough for me.

The next day I was rolling down the road with him in his big white 10-yard dump truck, towing the chipper behind us. It was a classic January morning in New England, with a bright blue sky and a constant soft wind blowing the freezing salt air into your bones. I was leaning up close to the heater in the truck, making fists to work-in the new pair of work gloves I bought on the way to work. But I was careful. I'd been through this before. I had the window rolled halfway down so I could still feel the cold air on me. I didn't want to get too comfortable. I wanted to be out and moving fast so I could show this guy how hard I could work; show him that I was tough like him and wasn't some kind of over-sensitive writer guy.

"So, what do you think of the operation?" he asked.

This was already the third time he'd asked me this question that morning. I had been with him approximately forty-five minutes. "Pretty good," I said.

He had his hard hat on with the ear protectors flipped up over the helmet like Mickey Mouse. He was leaning forward over the steering wheel with his eyes pinned about two inches away from the windshield, as if his posture would help him get to the job quicker. He was rocking back and forth slightly, almost imperceptibly.

"Yeah. They had this truck made especially for me," he said.

"Did they?" I questioned. I had seen a few others like it out on the roads. It didn't seem like anything crazy. It was just a ten-yard dump with a hard metal cover over the bed for holding chips.

"Well… not just for me. I bought it at a big tree show. They guy said there were only a few like it. This model. It was designed especially for tree professionals. I bought it from him on the spot. Cash. And had it shipped to my house. Or… driven. They drove it."

"Gotcha."

There was a brief moment of silence as Matt slowed down to make out a street sign, and wrenched at the wheel to guide us off the main road. I realized this was the first time he had stopped talking since we left his shop fifteen minutes ago. The silence felt nice, and I took a deep breath to enjoy it. We turned again and drove down a suburban side street lined with nice big houses with sprawling snow-covered lawns and two-car garages.

"Mmm-hmm!" Matt said affirmatively.

I wondered if I'd asked him something, but knew that I hadn't. "What?" I asked.

"How do you like the chipper?" he asked, ignoring my question completely.

"I don't know. I haven't used it yet. Seems pretty nice, though."

"Yeah. You'll like it. You just gotta get used to it. I'll show you. Do you do drugs?"

I looked over at him and he was pressed up close to the windshield, trying to look at house numbers while awaiting my reply. I chuckled at him and asked, "What do you got?"

"What?" he asked.

"Nothing. I'm good," I said.

"Well you can do drugs at Largess Forestry if you want. I had another writer named Bob and he liked to smoke pot all day. He was funny. 'Marijuana Bob' I used to call him. 456!" he called out, and mashed on the brakes.

I had to put my hands out on the glove compartment to brace myself.

"Mmm-hmm!" he repeated. He threw the truck in park, turned off the engine, and vaulted out of the truck all in the matter of a second. Then he hit the ground and without any break in his momentum he shifted his movement towards the front door of the house.

I laughed to myself in the confines of the truck while I watched him walk. He was like an industrial-sized tin-man, the way he walked leaning forward and the way his arms chugged away at his sides. Christ! He was making a beeline for the front door; practically running. He was on a mission.

Here's where I realized that I better get out and follow him, fast. I didn't know much about tree-work at all, but I knew enough about work-in-general to know that it's smart to follow the boss around closely on your first day in case he asks you to do something. So I got down out of the truck and hustled to catch up with him.

The lady of the house appeared out of her front door with her two young children just as Matt was nearly there. She was an attractive woman with long brown hair, wearing red lipstick and a fashionable jogging-suit of sorts. She seemed to be in a hurry. She smiled and said hi to Matt and then put her head down and focused it on the driver's side door of her SUV, which was running and all warmed-up in the driveway.

"Hey! Hi!" Matt called out jovially and continued barreling at her. "How's it going? Matt Largess, Largess Forestry at your service!"

"Oh... hi," she replied, looking towards her car like she'd rather just skip the conversation altogether. She wrapped her arms around herself and huddled up a bit, looking like she didn't really plan on being out in the cold too long in her jogging get-up, and perhaps eager to let it be known.

Matt didn't pick up on any of that. "Did you hear they found the ivory-billed woodpecker?" he asked.

"Excuse me?" she replied.

"The ivory-billed woodpecker. They found it down in the old-growth forest, down in White River National Wildlife Refuge in Arkansas. Did you hear about it?"

"No. I'm sorry. I haven't heard. I really don't—"

"No, huh? Wow. I'm surprised. That's really big news. It's been all over the newspapers, tv, radio... everything. I haven't been able to sleep for days. You know the story?"

The woman now took the time to really look at Matt for the first time, and allowed herself to laugh at him. Here was a man standing in front of her, looking genuinely and completely caught up in something she had never heard about in her entire life.

Matt laughed with her. "Yeah," he said. "I'm a real yahoo. Do you know the story, though?"

"No," answered the woman, beside herself, and surprised that she had offered him encouragement to continue. Now her and the two young boys were staring up at Matt with the same bewildered look on their faces.

"It's the Lord God Bird. It was thought to be extinct until they found it. A dead one. But newly dead... not that old. Found it in the same place I was looking. I *went* there, looking for it. And I swear I saw it but no one believed me because I didn't get a picture. And now they found it in the same place I was looking. It's very significant to science. Isn't that amazing?"

"Yes, it is," answered the woman, catching herself. "But... I'm sorry. I'm in kind of a rush. I have to get these guys to school."

"Oh. Hey guys. Hey little buddy," said Matt, addressing the older boy, who was probably around seven or eight.

The kid wasn't shy. Possibly, he sensed he could buy a few more minutes outside of the classroom if he played his cards right. "You're here to cut down some trees?" the boy asked him.

"Not cut them *down*. We're just here to prune them. I don't cut trees down unless there's a really good reason. I'm a preservationist. That's a big word for a kid like you. Ha! Tell 'em that one in school! Oh, people think I'm a real nut-job. I'll tell people to leave dead trees in their yards for wildlife habitat... put bat-houses up in the hollows and on the dead limbs. You have some beautiful trees on this property. They look nice and healthy for the most part. We're just doing a little bit of pruning to keep them growing right and let a little more light in the backyard. I have one of my guys on the way. Timmy. He's great. You'll love him. He's a great worker. And this is Shamus. He's a famous writer."

"Hi," I said.

I watched the two young boys shuffle slyly away from their mom while she was listening to Matt and start running around in the yard, their sneakers crunching through the crusty half-inch of snow on the front lawn.

"And we're feeding some of the trees, right?" Matt continued. "Microrisie. Deep-root feeding. It's similar to anthrax in the way it works. People don't like to hear that, but—"

"Oh! Boys!" hollered Mom, and gave Matt a look that said *Now you see what you've done?* "Come on. We're late. Stop that, now. Your feet will be soaked all day. Now come back here and get in the car." Then she turned back to Matt and said. "I'm sure it's all great... whatever you're doing... just do it. You already talked to my husband about all of it, right?"

"Frank?" Matt asked.

"Yes."

"Frank? Oh, yeah. He's a real good guy. A hot shit. He's into it. We got the whole thing all set. And your name is?"

"Oh... Melissa," she said shortly, sighing and showing Matt signs of her annoyance. "Billy! Jake! Come on, please! We're leaving right now!" And then to Matt she said, "I'm sorry. Whatever you talked about, then, just do it. I have some errands to run. You can leave the bill in the mailbox if I'm not back yet."

"Yeah, okay. I told Frank $1300 but I can make it $1150 if you want to pay cash. Cashola. How do you like that? We live in Rhode Island, right? Mobsters and lobsters. How ah ya? How ah ya?" Matt asked, doing his best impersonation of a Providence mobster.

"Oh, thanks," answered Melissa, now calling upon the last shreds of her patience. "But whatever you discussed in the first place is fine. Kids! Come on! Let's go!"

Matt turned to see the two boys pushing each other around near the corner of the house, by the air conditioner unit and the electric and gas meters. All at once his grinning face turned deadly serious. "HEY!" he bellowed. "YOU KIDS GET AWAY FROM THAT ELECTRIC BOX! THAT'S DANGEROUS!" Then he turned back to Melissa and told her, "I mean it. You have to keep these kids away from the electric box. That thing will take his head clean *off*!"

Both her and her kids stood astonished in the front yard, stunned by the sudden change in his disposition.

Then Matt caught a glimpse of something over Melissa's shoulder and all traces of concern left his face. "Ooh! Turkey Oak," he announced pleasantly, and began walking off to the far corner of the property. "It's a beautiful specimen... if that's what it really is. Rare around these parts. You don't usually see..." his voice trailed off as he rounded the corner of the house, leaving Melissa standing and looking at me, wondering what the hell had just happened to her.

"Don't worry about it," I told her. "We do nice work."

I walked back to the truck and found the compartment where Matt kept his chain saws. Then I laid one out on the ground and made like I was fiddling with the thing while she pulled away so she could see at least one of us doing something that resembled work. Matt was still out back, looking up into the leafless winter canopy in the small patch of woods to the rear of her property.

CHAPTER 2

(Into the way, way-back machine)

The river was rolling gently now, lapping up against the smooth boulders along the banks and rushing silently around the base of the kayak. Thirteen-year-old Matthew Largess leaned back in the boat with his paddle out of the water, resting across his thighs. He was a skinny little boy with a full head of brown hair that flapped wildly in the wind. There was only the slightest hint of the future fire hydrant-frame developing in his boyish torso. Matt had unusually broad shoulders for a schoolboy. It was early summer. The sun shone down from the sky and warmed the skin on his face and arms while the gentle wind blew along the river and kept him cool. There was no sound except the rushing of the water and the wind blowing through the trees that extended for miles along both banks of the river.

There was a smell to it, too. There was the fresh, clean smell of the river, far different from the slow-moving swamp-like streams he played in back home in Rhode

Island. There were no pockets of lily pads, no pools of stagnant black water that smelled of muck and mildew. The water here was constantly moving. It was a rolling steel blue with a pure scent. Coupled with the smell of the river was the smell of the forest. There was a slightly earthy part to it; maybe the leaves of years past decaying on the forest floor. He recognized that part from the woods back home in the early springtime. Then there was the smell of the bark, of the sap in the pines, and of the new glossy maple leaves that were yet to be scorched by the summer sun.

He floated wherever the river took him. When it took him into a patch of rocks or too close to the shore he would stick his paddle against the obstruction and shove off back towards the center of the river. He had lost sight of the others in front of him long ago, around a lazy bend in the river. He came on this trip with a friend from school and his friend's family, the Vierra family. During the final hours of the long car ride out to Pennsylvania he started to think he had made a mistake by agreeing to come. Seven hours in a car to go *camping*? Couldn't they just do that in his back yard? What was the big deal about it, anyway? And now, as he leaned back in the kayak and let the river take him, he saw the difference.

He thought he had been in the woods before. There was the stretch of woods behind the elementary school in Jamestown where he and his friends would play manhunt and hide-and-go- seek. Back then, it seemed like those woods were bigger than the world. Now he was old enough to realize that there was a neighborhood that bordered the whole thing. It was only a couple acres, tops. Out here...

there was nothing. He thought of the term "wilderness" from one of his textbooks and made the connection. When they were talking about the Indians in the wilderness, they were not talking about the trees behind the elementary school, as he once thought as a child. They were talking about something more like this; about something that had never been built upon, about a place where you couldn't hear the sound of cars going by off in the distance or of afternoon church bells ringing. They were talking about a place like this.

Did everyone know that there were still places like this? If they did, why hadn't anyone told him about it before? Why hadn't anyone shown him?

A sharp, cracking sound came from the direction of one of the riverbanks and snapped Matt out of his meditations. He looked up to the shore to see what could possibly interrupt the quiet flow of the river and found some movement there. It was a deer, walking gingerly down to the water to get a drink. The loud snap was just the deer stepping on a broken branch that lay on the ground. It was a bony, wild female with black eyes and a tuft of white hair on her behind. The doe saw Matt and looked at him with those black eyes, *watched* him for a few seconds, and then continued down towards the river.

Matt smiled. *She knows I'm all right,* he thought. *She knows that I get it.* He was exhilarated for a moment, just as he was yesterday when he pulled his first trout out of the river. He was so exited when he got the fish into his boat that he almost rolled it and returned them both back into the water. He remembered holding the wet, cold fish in his hands and watching the color play along its scales while it wriggled back and forth in the sun. Seeing the deer was kind of the same thing. Even the forest, the way the trees swayed around and were alive, that was kind of the same thing, too.

As the wind shifted and blew Matt's hair back out of his eyes and off his forehead, he heard the faint sound of human voices off in the distance. It sounded strange and out of place to him at first; for a while he imagined himself to be completely alone. But then it became more familiar. It was Tommy Vierra and his dad, calling for him. They must be worried about him by now. He figured he'd better start paddling and catch up to them so they'd know he was okay. *Funny,* Matt thought as he dipped one end of his paddle into the water and pulled back, causing the kayak to lurch forward, *I wasn't even scared at being left behind, all alone out here. I think I'm even happier than I've ever been in my life.*

CHAPTER 3

(Into the way-back machine)

The campus of Paul Smith College was the largest in land area in the entire United States. 55,000 acres of forest in the Adirondack Mountains of upstate New York served as the learning grounds where young students of forestry studied dendrology, forest management, milling lumber, proper pruning, and everything else you could ever want to know about trees. The education focused on both the science of the forest and the practices that were used in the field. Students took tests in classrooms and were evaluated on cutting trees on the sides of wild mountainsides. Some students took more to the practical side of the education and some took more to the scientific aspect. And some students learned in a different way altogether.

Young Matthew Largess often boasted of his education, "I minor in air products and major in space." No one really had any idea what he was talking about most of the time he said that, but it didn't matter much to Matt. He was too stoned all the time to pay much attention to other people's reactions to things. He was having enough trouble managing all the stray thoughts, cosmic rumblings, and primal urges that constantly raged against one another in his own mind without having to worry about other people. That was a full time job in itself.

"I minor in air products and major in space," Matt told the young lady inside The Bear Trap in Saranac Lake, New York. Saranac Lake was located only a few miles from the campus of Paul Smith College and offered a wide variety of watering holes where students could cut loose from the rigors of formal education. The drinking age in 1969 was 18, so booze formed a common bond between underclassmen and seniors alike. Paul Smith College didn't need fraternities or sororities. It had the bars of Saranac Lake.

"What are you? Some kind of astronaut?" the young lady asked Matt sarcastically, sucking gin and tonic through a straw between a buffer of full lips painted with hot red lipstick. She was a semi-attractive yet disinterested girl of about nineteen or twenty years of age. She wore a heavy coat of make-up and tight clothing; jeans and a pale blue sweater that showed-off every inch of her fullness. She was somewhere between being full-bodied and chubby. Her blonde hair was cut shoulder-length and slicked off to the side.

Matt realized that this girl was not one of his fellow students of forestry. This was something far different from the long hair, hiking boots, and handmade dresses-over-jeans look that dominated the female fashion scene of Paul Smith. This girl was local. Matt decided to go with it.

"Yup," he told her. "I'm going to the moon, baby. Straight to the moon. I'll probably be up there in five years, if everything goes right. After my training is over. What's your name?"

"Diana," said the girl, sucking on her straw and looking around at the crowd over Matt's shoulder.

The Bear Trap was a small, dark smoky bar with low ceilings. It was Friday night, so all the tables and chairs were piled up against one wall to make room for more bodies. Most of the college kids were standing around in small groups in the middle of the bar. The local after-work drinkers held steadfastly to their bar-seats, and a small crowd was gathered around the jukebox, watching a pair of drunken girls twirl each other around off-rhythm to the hum of an old country tune.

Matt looked down at his half-full beer and then drained the rest of it. "Can I buy you a drink?" he asked.

The girl smiled and looked at him full in the face for the first time, showing her yellow-stained teeth and a trace of the innocent young girl she had once been. "You got money, college boy?"

"Sure." Matt smiled back at her.

The girl bent her forefinger and gestured for Matt to come closer. When he did, she grabbed his shirt and gently pulled him close to her, close enough so he could feel her weighty breasts pressing up against his chest. She put her painted red lips close to his ear so he could feel her breath and whispered, "For thirty dollars you can take me back in the storage room and do anything you want with me."

"Really?" Matt asked, delighted. "Thirty bucks! That's unbelievable! That's great!"

The girl nodded affirmatively. She pulled out a pack of smokes from her purse and lit one up. "It's usually thirty-five. But I like you. You're handsome. Strong. Not Flabby." She reached out her hand and rubbed Matt's chest lightly. "So what do you say?"

"I say 'let's go'!"

The girl stood up and took Matt's hand. She led him through the crowded barroom and down the back hallway, out of the smoky light of the barroom and into the shadows of the storage room, behind closed doors and amidst the clutter of cardboard boxes.

❧

He lived in White Pine Camp. It was an old forestry camp way down a long dirt road that stretched from the classrooms into the depths of the wilderness. There was a cluster of old log cabins down there that used to house the loggers when they first harvested timber from the mountainside years ago. Now new trees had grown in their place and students had replaced the pioneers of this land. The students of White Pine Camp comprised the wildest crew in the entire school. They had a theory that the school officials intentionally lumped them together and sent them as far away from the center of campus as possible, hoping to keep the corruption of the other students to a minimum.

A walking-tour through the camp on a Saturday morning in early fall of Matt's junior year showed you everything you needed to know. There were remnants of a few campfires still smoldering in the morning light. Empty whiskey bottles and beer bottles littered the outskirts of the campfires. A raccoon-skin hat lay on the ground like a dead carcass, abandoned by its owner the night before. Outside of Matt's cabin there was an interesting gathering of clutter. There was a chain saw in pieces on the ground next to empty oil cans and a half-full container of gasoline. Two hunting rifles leaned up against the side of the cabin. There was a large hunting knife sticking straight out of the timbers next to the door, surrounded by hundreds of hack-marks from where it had been tossed in the past.

The door was half open. Matt lay face-down on the cold wood floor just inside, shirtless and with his pants down around his ankles. He was bare-ass. He clutched onto the base of a fifth of Jack Daniels with about an inch of brown liquor left in the bottom. He had a strong, broad back and the muscles around his left shoulder stood out from the pressure with which he gripped the bottle.

Matt opened one eye and watched the blurry colors come into focus. He smiled at the bottle of Jack staring back at him and chuckled. "I didn't spill a drop," he said out loud. He shifted his weight and felt the dirt grinding underneath his bare body on the surface of the wood floor, and looked down.

"What the...?" he asked himself, wondering how he ended up with his pants down. What was the last thing he remembered? Oooh. He better not go there. He could have sworn the sun was shining the last time he was awake. It was probably another solid eight-hour blackout.

Matt chuckled. He let go of the bottle, got onto his feet and pulled his pants up. A ripping pain shot through his temple, and he clutched at his head. He saw the big mop of brown hair buried in the pillow a few feet away from him on the couch. That was his roommate, Pete Scholla; his best buddy in the whole world. Pete was huddled under a blanket, sleeping face down.

"Pete. You didn't rape me last night, did you?" Matt asked.

Pete groaned something inarticulate into the pillow without moving.

"Did I get laid?" Matt asked.

More groaning.

"Well… whatever," Matt concluded. He walked heavily through the clutter of dirty dishes, notebooks and album covers of the common room into the clutter of dirty clothes in his small bedroom. Matt opened up the top drawer and stared pleasantly inside. The entire drawer was filled to the top with fresh marijuana buds. It was his stash for the whole semester… or as long as it lasted. He broke off a piece of a nice fragrant bud and put it in the bong that he kept on his bedside table. He pulled tube after tube of the light, creamy smoke and stared out the paneled window until he felt it hit him.

A rush of memories flooded his mind all at once. He remembered waking up in this room last winter when it was thirty degrees below zero, throwing a pail of water out this window and hearing it CRACK when it hit the air. He remembered Professor Koudesh lecturing the class on the make-up of the underbrush on the forest floor. They were out in the woods, standing on a layer of brown pine needles that had fallen off the big white pines. He remembered banging that girl on the stack of cardboard boxes in the storage room. The corner of a box of Miller High Life was digging into his thigh. "The champagne of beers," it boasted in green lettering underneath the logo. And the look on his girl's face was just as disinterested as it was when he first approached her. He remembered the complete silence he heard when he hiked the Forty-Sixers by himself the previous Fall. After time, the silence seemed to take on a noise more powerful than sound. He had to clutch onto the stem of a sapling to keep himself from being blown away by it.

Matt snapped back into reality to find himself clutching onto his bedpost just as he had clutched onto the sapling. He flinched and his knees buckled, sending him half to the ground before he recovered. A wave of paranoia came over him. That wasn't right. The human mind was not supposed to work like that. That was scary.

Then he smiled. He grabbed the bong and went right back at it, eager to see if he could make it happen again.

CHAPTER 4

"So, how do you like the operation?" Matt asked me.

We were sitting in his little Dodge truck at lunch time, parked in front of a job. It was an unusually warm day for the middle of winter, with the sun shining and melting the snow. The pavement was covered with sand and muddy puddles and the snow was wet and heavy on the lawn where I was dragging brush. My beat-up work boots were soaked clean through with the mush.

"Pretty good," I told him. The job really wasn't that bad. I had been prepared for the worst because the only other job I had doing tree work was brutal. I was lifting huge rounds of wood all day and I swear it strained my nuts from all the effort. I could barely walk after the day's work. But with Matt, there was none of that. Mainly all he did was pruning, so there were no huge rounds to lug around. We *had* taken down a couple of dead ones that were pretty beefy, but at least I wasn't straining nuts every day. It was bearable.

"Yeah? What do you think? You like the chipper?"

"I love the chipper," I lied. The thing worked fine; I had no problem with that. It was just way too loud for me. It was so loud, even with the hard hat and the ear protectors on, that my brain wasn't capable of functioning properly while it was running. It was violently loud. Every now and then I would shove a branch into the thing and then go reeling away from it in some random direction, probably subconsciously from wanting to be away from it as soon as possible. Sometimes I'd walk straight into some bushes and get all tangled up, other times I'd wander off into the road. I could see how guys got flattened by passing cars on the job. Only pure luck separated me from the flattened. I had to work on that.

"Yeah? Good. I got a lot of work. Is your wife pregnant?"

I was a bit startled by the question, wondering how he knew about it. Then I realized I mentioned it to the guys on his crew, and didn't tell them not to tell anyone or anything. "Well… no one's really supposed to know, yet. It's still early. But no one I know really knows you, so… yeah," I told him.

"Wow! That's great!" he said.

"Yeah," I said. "I guess it's a little sooner than I—"

"Now you gotta work! Work, work, work! Right?"

I laughed. "I guess so."

"You bet your ass. Great! I need you. I just got a call from this big-time development company. They want to clear some land in Portsmouth. It could be big. Weeks… months… thousands and thousands of dollars. I'm going to look at it today. I should go right now. I will. I'll go right away. Okay, get out. You probably want a raise. That's okay. It's good to have somebody who knows what they're doing," he said.

Does he really think I know what I'm doing?, I wondered. I mean, I could drag brush all day with the best of them and I could run a chain saw as long as I was standing on the ground. But I didn't know how to tie a knot to save my life, I couldn't climb trees, I was constantly getting in the way of the other guys on the crew, and there was the whole wandering-into-the-road thing.

"I bet," I said. "It's tough to find good help these days."

"It is," he said. "And you got a kid on the way. I'll give you ninety a day. Cash. That's—"

"I was hoping for more like a hundred," I announced loudly, giving him a taste of his own medicine by cutting him off. I figured I might as well push the limit as long as we were talking money. I'd learned over the years that people don't like to concede things unless you ask for them, and often find it hard to say no when they're put on the spot.

"Hmmm," he said.

"My last job, landscaping out on Martha's Vineyard, I was making 18 an hour," I told him.

"Yeah. But a hundred a day.... Cash... that's as much as Weeman makes. And he's been working for me for two years."

"He's an illegal alien," I said. "You don't even have to pay him if you don't want to."

Matt laughed maniacally. "You're right! I should stiff him this week! He'd kill me. He hates me, doesn't he? The Weeman?" he asked, seeming genuinely concerned.

"I think he's just playing," I told him.

"Yeah. We go at it pretty good, me and the Weeman. Don't we?"

"Yeah. What about the money. Is that cool?"

"Yeah, yeah. Fine. A hundred a day. And it's only 'til the spring and then you'll do your own thing with the landscaping. Maybe you'll work for me a couple days a week until you get it going. You're a good guy. I like you. You're smart," he said.

"Thanks," I said. "Good luck in Portsmouth," I told him.

I got out of the truck and strutted triumphantly through the wet snow into the backyard where Tim and Weeman were relaxing at the end of our lunch break. My cold, soaking feet and pants-legs weren't bothering me as much now, now that I knew I was worth more. Even though I realized full well that it didn't matter. A hundred a day still wasn't enough. Maybe enough for a twenty-six year-old booze-bag whose favorite thing to do was to stay home all day and write books that made him zero dollars. But not enough for the booze-bag and his wife and kid. But I'd been thinking about that enough, lately. For now, I allowed myself to block it out and feel proud of my petty negotiating skills.

Tim was sitting about ten feet off the ground in the lowest notch of an eighty-year-old beech tree, still attached to his rope and climbing harness. He was packing a big plug of Skoal in his bottom lip.

"So, how do you like the operation?" he asked, and dropped a big brown loogey down into the trampled snow around the base of the tree.

"Uhmm... pretty good," I said.

Tim laughed. "Just kidding," he said. "How many times did Mickey ask you that just now?"

"Mickey?" I asked.

"Yeah, Matt. That's one of his nicknames... the one I like to call him."

"Oh," I said. Then I thought about it. "How come?"

"I'm not really sure. He just kind of came with it. Maybe it's because he flips the ear protectors up on his helmet and looks like Mickey Mouse. So how many times did he ask you?"

"Probably about twelve," I said. "And that's just today."

Tim laughed again. He was a short, stocky blonde kid about my age with an all-American boy's regular haircut. He was really wide and strong and into being in shape. He talked about the gym all the time and could climb up a rope like there were jets on his back. Tim also liked his booze, and for that reason we'd be as good as brothers.

"Fuckin' Mickey," Weeman piped in with his Scottish accent. "He'll be pounding my brain all day long with that. 'How do you like the operation... how do you like the operation... Shut the fuck up!"

"Right," I said.

Weeman's real name was Dominic and he stood about 5'2". He had sandy blonde hair and pale blue eyes like Matt's, only without the fireworks show. His shoulders were broad but he was fairly slight of frame, otherwise. Except for his beer belly, which was formidable. He never stopped moving once we were working. If there was no more brush to drag he'd be at the rake, or picking up the tiniest of sticks just to keep from being idle. And he had a strength within him that was completely disproportionate to his frame.

I don't really consider myself a tough guy for the most part, but sometimes I like to. I'm six feet tall and I'm young and healthy and I'm certainly no weakling. I was pretty good at sports and all that. But the other day on the job I was struggling to get a big chunk of dead pine into the back of the one-ton dump truck. I kind of picked it up a little and then gave up on it, thinking it would be easier with two people. Weeman came over to it and grappled the thing (it was nearly as big as him when he was doubled over) stood up and flung it over his shoulder into the bed of the truck. Then he winked at me and lit up a cigarette with a theatric flourish.

"Mickey's taken a real liking to you, hasn't he?" he asked, smiling. He was sitting on top of a bed of downed branches, keeping his ass up off the wet snow.

"I guess so," I said, a bit defensively. I couldn't tell by his tone if he was jealous or not.

"That's good," said Tim. "That means me and Weeman don't have to ride with him as much."

"Aye," said Weeman.

"How about this one. How about when there's a second of silence, and he'll be sitting there and going, 'Mmmhmm. Mmmhmm. Mmmhmm!'"

I laughed. "Yeah," I said. "That's a good one. It's like he can't handle the silence at all... like he's compulsive about talking. It's pretty... insane. Maybe OCD or something."

"It's funny you use that word. You know he *was* insane once... like in some kind of institution and everything," said Tim.

"Really?" I asked.

"Yeah. I don't think it was a full-blown insane asylum. I think it was more like a drug-rehab place, with like a looney-bin wing to it or something."

"Wow," I said. "How do you know that?"

Tim laughed. "He told me. He doesn't give a shit. Ask him. He'll tell you all about it. He said he woke up every day for like two months thinking he was getting ready for some kind of speech."

CHAPTER 5

(into the twilight zone of the past)

"Good morning, Matthew," said the nurse upon entering Matt's suite. She was a handsome, middle-aged woman with soft brown hair and shiny rose-colored lipstick. She wore a traditional white-on-white, starched nurse's uniform with a crisp white hat riding a wave of hair spray on the crown of her head.

Matt looked up from his notebook and searched her face. He found her vaguely familiar, and smiled. The room, too had that same sense to it, like he knew it but was seeing it all for the first time in a very long time. One wall was all windows, looking out onto a sprawling lawn leading down to a dark pond outlined by small brush and smattered with lily pads. The room seemed like a college common-room of sorts, with generic cheaply made furniture and shelves full of outdated books. The dusty, morning light played through the wall of windows and added to the surreal effect. He was laying in an adjustable bed with his back propped up for reading and he had the sheets pulled up to his waist.

"Hey!" Matt announced pleasantly. "How's it going?"

"Oh. Just fine, thank you. And how's it going with you this morning? I see you're working on something, there," she said, gesturing towards his notebook.

"Mmmhmm! Just getting ready for my speech… going over some notes," he answered, and began rifling back through pages, as if he had just remembered something.

"I see," said the nurse, and frowned. "And what will you be speaking on, and where, if you don't mind me asking again?"

"No. Hell no! I don't mind. Of course not." Matt reached his hand up to scratch his head and played with some long tufts of wavy brown hair. It was funny… it was much longer than he remembered. He stretched it down in front of his eyes and looked at it strangely.

"I'm sorry," said the nurse. "If you don't feel like talking about it…"

"No. It's just…" Matt looked down and flipped absently through some pages of the notebook. "You know… I really can't remember for the life of me right now. I know it's going to be at some kind of university… and… soon. And… it must be about trees… and forestry. That's what I always talk about. I'm a good speaker. That's what I'm good at: talking. People like to listen to me. Although… I don't remember what aspect. Are we there right now? Am I here? At the college?"

The nurse smiled compassionately. "You're still confused. Perhaps you'd like some breakfast? Are you hungry?"

"Yeah!" he roared. "That's it! I haven't had my coffee yet! I'm nothing without it. Can't think straight. I'd love some coffee. And toast, eggs… whatever you got."

Matt looked down at his notebook again and noticed the shirt he was wearing. It wasn't his... it was like... a hospital shirt or something. It was one of those thin aqua blue, short-sleeve numbers.

"Where's my clothes? Are my clothes here?" he asked.

"Yes, they're here. You're just resting for a moment."

"Oh, okay," Matt said, relieved. "I wouldn't be able to go to my speech like this. I need... my clothes. Is this place like... a hospital or something?"

"Yes," said the nurse and nodded. "It is. It's nothing to be alarmed about. You had an accident and suffered some trauma... it's nothing physical, you understand. You are physically fit. You're just resting, right now. This is a good place. It's clean and it's safe and everything will be taken care of for you."

"Oh," Matt answered, sounding disappointed. He looked out the window and saw an evergreen not far from the building, and quickly studied its shape and form. He saw the coloring, the cones, and the clustering of the needles and recognized it as a small Douglas Fir. "Are we in Oregon?" he asked.

"Yes," answered the nurse, seeming impressed. "That's very good."

"Good. That must be where I'm speaking, then. At Oregon State University. I think. Hey... you said there's nothing *physically* wrong with me. Is this some kind of psycho-ward? Like in Kesey's book? I know him, you know. I've been to his place... partied with him and everything. We're like buddies... well not *buddies* but he'd know me if he saw me. Is that what this place is?"

"Matthew," the nurse said soothingly. "Please don't work yourself up. You're resting, now. Remember that above everything else. This is not a 'psycho-ward' as you say. This is a place where you can rest. Just... focus on your speech if that's what helps you," she said, and showed her first sign of being flustered just before she turned to exit the room. "I'll be right back with your breakfast," she announced on her way out.

That left Matt alone with his thoughts and his notebook. He looked down and concentrated on the words written on the page in front of him. There weren't many. It said, in his own sprawling handwriting that only he could decipher: DENDROLOGY. TREE RINGS. INSTINCTS. STATEWIDE MANHUNT FOR SPECIES. INSECTS. DISEASES. The words were set apart from each other on different lines and decorated with squiggles, arrows leading nowhere, and primitive stick drawings. Matt touched the pen to the paper and wrote anew towards the bottom of the page: OREGON. CONCENTRATE ON SPECIES OF THE NORTHWEST. Then he set his pen down and stretched, arching his arms behind his back, satisfied with his progress.

CHAPTER 6

Matt was aware that someone was talking to him as he was walking through the stand of woods known commonly as Oakland Forest, although he was trying to block out the words in order to get better in tune with the feeling that the forest was pumping into him. It was a cold, gray February afternoon. His breath funneled out through his mouth and nose in escalated bursts, rising up towards the outstretched limbs of the beech trees before mingling in with the gray air. The copper-colored leaves that clung to the low branches of the beeches were the only splashes of color in the landscape.

The beeches dominated over all the other species, and they were large for growing wild in a wooded area like this. There were bigger ones on some of the mansions around Newport, but that was because there were only one or two of them on the whole property. The root system only had to support a single tree. Here there was a network. There was a staggered but systematic placement of trees and a pattern of small suckering growth that shot up from the root system here and there. He recognized the high canopy and the relative absence of brush. It was all open in there, with a nice, high ceiling of outstretched limbs. It meant that this was possibly an old growth forest; something that had never been cut by man. There were some giant White Oaks too, some of the biggest he had seen in anywhere in Rhode Island.

But it was more than just the trees that were blowing him away. There was something about this place. He had been around big trees before and never felt like this. He felt like his spirit was about to lift out of his body and fly away. It was like… religious… or something. It was like the way church *should* have felt to him if it worked the way it worked for other people. At least, this is how he imagined it should feel.

Matt turned and looked at the man who was walking next to him, acknowledging his presence for the first time in minutes. He was one of the guys from the development group. Jim Trent was his name. He seemed like a pretty good guy. He was friendly enough. Guessing from the way he was dressed, he wasn't much of an outdoors-man. He had on a long gray wool trench coat, slacks and new white sneakers. He was a young-looking guy in his early forties, with a skinny freshly-shaven face. His cheeks were whipped red by the winter breeze. He had dark eyes, almost black, framed by thick-rimmed retro glasses.

"Out on this perimeter here is where the western reach of the access road would be," he continued, looking down at his blueprints and up again through the woods. "We want to leave enough of a buffer strip between the units and the highway so it seems like you're still out here in the woods. We want to keep that feel, if we can."

"Mmmhmm," said Matt. "You're a smart guy. All you guys are smart. All you guys that I've talked to. What are you? Ivy League or something? Brown?"

Jim smiled at him. "Yale, actually," he said.

"No shit? That's great. That's really... great," Matt said, his voice trailing off.

Jim went on talking about his plans, gesturing from the blueprints up to the wilderness. As they walked, other sounds began to mingle in with the sound of Jim's voice. These weren't sounds that were actually coming from the forest on that cold winter day; they were sounds from a distant time and place. There were sounds of chain saws running, sounds of gruff men talking crudely and slapping each other on the back, and the sound of helicopters whirling above him. These new sounds became stronger and stronger until they took over completely and Jim's voice didn't exist. And neither did the forest they were walking in.

Matt saw himself standing at the outskirts of the logging camp twenty years earlier, looking back at the land they had just cleared in the previous weeks. He held his saw with the four-foot bar down by his waist, the motor resting on his thighs and the bar pointed across his body. There were men behind him on their lunch break, talking about finding a whore to have sent into camp that night. A helicopter was headed away from the camp, the last traces of its hurricane winds rustling the tops of the redwoods.

He was positioned on the crest of a steep hill and could see for what appeared to be miles back in the direction from which they'd come. And all across that land there was nothing. There was no life there. It was dead. All that remained were stumps, sawdust, tire tracks, and flattened clumps of underbrush. He could see it all exactly, down to the most minute detail, even the way the tips of the leaves on the underbrush closest to him were wilted brown; ready to die and blend in with the rest of the carnage.

He remembered this moment so clearly because it was one of the only moments of clarity in his drug and alcohol-crazed, outside-the-land-of-the-law years he spent in the Oregon wilderness. It was like a switch was flipped inside his brain. It was the first time in his life that he had ever wondered if what he was doing was right. The thought had simply never occurred to him before. It was work. Work was work. And this was bad-ass work. But now, looking back over the wreckage of his labor, he wondered how long it would take that forest to grow back. He wondered if it would ever be capable of getting back to where it was. 1400 years. That's how old they said some of these trees were. That was a long time. That was---

"Mr. Largess? Matt! Are you with me?" came the sound of the developer's voice, snapping Matt back into the present.

"Am I with you?" he asked.

"Yeah," responded Jim, with a strange smile. "You weren't saying anything. Seems like I lost you, there for a second."

"Nah. You're fine. Let me ask you something, though," said Matt.

"Sure. Go ahead."

Matt looked down at the ground and played with some of the matted beech leaves on the path with the tip of his boot. He thought one more time about the thousands of dollars he was about to piss away with his next comment, thought better of it, and then resigned because he knew his mind was made up already.

"You ever thought about saving this place?" he asked.

"Saving it?" asked Jim, letting the plans fall down to his waist with a crumple-crinkle of papers. "What do you mean, *saving* it?"

"You know. Like... not cutting any of it. Scrapping the whole project. Just leaving the trees and this whole forest how it is so people can come here and enjoy it. This is like the only stretch of woods left around here. And I think this is really old. It looks like it may have never been cut—ever. Do you know how important that is to nature... to the ecosystem... if that's really the case?"

"No," said Jim. Now he snapped his plans open and began rolling them up to put them away. "No and no," he said. "No, I've never thought about *saving* these trees because I'm a *developer.* That's my job and that's what I do. That's how I make my money and that's how my family eats. Kind of like you're a tree guy, and your job is to cut trees. That's how *you* make money. That's what you do; or so I thought. I *develop* the land. I do not *leave it alone forever.* That's the opposite of development. That's stagnation. That's... waste. And no, I don't know how important that is to nature. And while I'm sympathetic, I don't really care because it's not my job to care."

"Aw, man," said Matt. "You don't have to get mad at me. I was just asking."

"Yeah. Well... look. I appreciate where you're coming from and everything, but look at it from my perspective," said Jim, maintaining a calm tone. "I, or my partners and I, bought this land for... a certain large sum of money. We came up with this plan. We crunched the numbers. We need to build 52 condos and sell them for $770,000 each to be able to make the necessary profit. It's all math. It's business. To just do nothing with this land, to *eat the money*, is not an option, however noble it may be."

"I hear you," said Matt. "But maybe you wouldn't have to eat it. They have agencies that buy up pieces of land like this. Like nature conservancies and stuff."

"Yeah. That's not making a profit," Jim scoffed. "That's taking a loss for no reason. It's poor business. Look," he said. He sighed and looked around at the woods before he continued. "I wish you didn't wait until we got a mile out into the woods to start pulling this. The fact of the matter is: we're going to get this land cleared whether you do it or not. We'll find somebody else—easy. But, I mean... you saw the plans. We're not cutting *everything*. We're leaving what we can, besides the roads and the units, and small common areas."

"I've seen the plans," Matt said complacently. "They're good plans. Everything looks beautiful. I told you; you guys are smart guys. I like you. But you *are* clearing the majority of it. And what's left is never going to be the same, trust me. It'll probably all die off in a few years because you're disrupting—"

"So you don't want to do it?" Jim interrupted, looking Matt in the eye. "Is that what you're telling me?"

Matt looked away from him, looked up into the canopy and at the tree trunks around him. He thought one more time about the sweet money this job would bring in before he kissed it goodbye; about college funds for his boys, the big tree spade truck he had his eye on, renovating the bathroom, mortgage payments, a retirement fund… all that good stuff. But who cared? There wasn't any way to get ahead, anyway.

"I guess I don't," Matt told him. "And I'm serious about saving this place. I'm going to get back to you about some other options. You never know, maybe you'll end up changing your mind."

"That's fine, if that's what you want to do. But I can tell you right now it'll be a complete waste of time. We have our mind made up. This is going to happen, whether you like it or not," Jim answered.

"It's not really about me," said Matt. "Well, come on. We're gonna walk out together. We might as well be nice to each other. I don't have any hard feelings toward you or anything."

"No," Jim said. "Likewise."

"Yeah. What the hell? What's the use in that?" Matt responded, as the two started walking back towards their vehicles.

Jim chuckled. "True."

"Good. I might as well talk to you about this place. I know every tree in this place. Every species… everything. I'll show you the pattern of old growth that I recognize.

There's a mother beech somewhere around here. I haven't seen it yet. Hey! Maybe we could walk around and..."

Here Matt paused and looked over at Jim, who was staring back at him with a raised eyebrow to make it plain that he truly could care less.

"Right," Matt continued. "Anyway, what happens is, the mother tree is the center of the whole network, and everything else shoots off of that. It's all connected. The entire root system. I'll show you. You can see some of the off-shoots on our way back."

"Great," Jim said sarcastically, and thought to himself: *Wow. This is going to be a long walk back.*

CHAPTER 7

(back into the heart of destruction)

Twenty-eight year old Matt largess came storming out from the pisser inside The Gearbox, frantically rubbing his red nose and eyes which were on fire from the rails of cocaine he'd just snorted off the top of the urinal. His hair was wild and greasy, mussed about in every direction from not showering and grabbing fist-fulls of it and wrenching it around. He was built like a linebacker in these days, and he walked with the hard confidence of a coke-faced man who's fairly certain he could kick the shit out of just about any man in the bar to begin with.

The Gearbox was a makeshift log cabin of a watering hole built hastily in the foothills of the mountains at the edge of civilization. It was constructed *by* a retired employee of the logging operation *for* use by other employees of the camp; a crude construction of roughly milled lumber and heavy lacquer. It was as open as a banquet hall except for the horseshoe bar near the entrance. Most of the tables and chairs had been busted apart in brawls and the rest were removed in a conscientious effort to get rid of any unnecessary objects that were capable of killing a man when swung with enough force.

Needless to say, the men of the camp drank to excess when they got the chance to come to The Gearbox. Often, it would be their first chance at debauchery after weeks of working their lives away out in the woods. True, some of them brought bottles and flasks out there with them, but those didn't last long. A trip to the Gearbox also marked their re-entry into civilization. A tiny little hick town in northern Oregon was no Big Apple, but it did have things like a stores, women and police, none of which they had out at camp. Being back in society was cause for celebration, almost like being let out of prison. It was party-time.

Matt thundered across the plank-wood floor on the way to his barstool, hollering, "Whoo! Whoo! Yeah, baby! Yeah! Let's go, now! Yeah!" The remarks were made to no one in particular, and none of the patrons that he passed on his way took any exceptional notice to his rant. At last he arrived at his barstool and slipped his arm around the slender back of the hot young blonde seated next to him. Tina was her name. She was the wife of one of the helicopter pilots that Matt worked with. The guy, Roger, was nowhere in sight and Matt wasn't about to ask any questions, especially when she rubbed her hands up and down his thighs underneath the bar.

Ol' Roger will be dead before any of us anyway, Matt mused with a complete lack of remorse. It was true. The pilots had it the worst. Of the seven original pilots that started the operation, only five were left. Roger was one of the replacements. You see, the entire thing was an experiment. This kind of thing had never been done before. It was trial and error. How many logs could you lift off the ground without crashing and burning? How did the weather and the wind affect it? It was all guesswork. And when the pilots guessed wrong, they died. Even when they had it down pat, something weird would happen. Like a mechanical problem or a snag in one of the grappling lines.

Matt worked underneath the birds, sawing up the logs and getting the grappling wire around them for lift-off. Men had died doing his job, too, but it wasn't as bad as being a pilot. The easiest way to die on Matt's job was to be smashed to death by an airborne log that had been sucked off the ground by the helicopters as they powered up to take off. Another way was to be crushed by the helicopters when they made their crash landing; of course that way wasn't too promising for the pilots, either. These were all ways to die, as were heart attacks, cancer and being hit by a truck while crossing the street. To Matt it was all the same. Everyone had to go somehow. He might as well spend his days doing something that let him know he was living.

Matt smelled the flowery shampoo on Tina's golden hair as she leaned in close to him on her barstool and was aroused by the memories that the scent produced. He remembered a few weeks ago when it happened for the first time, skidding her across the hard, mat-like rug on her living room floor. Neither of them noticed the layers of skin they had rug-burned off in the effort until it was all over. It was that good.

"We can go whenever you want," Tina whispered to him. "Roger is away, again. He'll be gone all weekend."

"Yeah, yeah," Matt answered coldly, nudging her away with his elbow. His lust subsided as quickly as it devoured him. That was all fine and good, but if she was going to try to cut into his drinking time she could go screw herself. And he could find somebody else.

"Hey! Toby! Toby!" Matt called out in the direction of the bartender, who was busy in conversation with another customer.

"Will you hold on a damn minute!" Toby snapped back. He was a white-haired man with a tired face and tattoos on his forearms, which exploded from the short-sleeves of his collared shirt. Toby worked as a topper until the arthritis wouldn't let him close his hands tightly enough to grip his saw or the branches of the redwoods as he made his way up to their tops into the sky. For this, he had the respect of most of the men that frequented The Gearbox. To Matt, he was a second-rate bartender and nothing more.

Matt gnashed his teeth together and pounded on the bar with his fist, waiting for him to come down. Punctuality; that was Toby's main problem. A man should have a fresh drink waiting for him before his first glass was empty. After what seemed to him like an eternity, he finally shuffled his way down.

"Good," Matt said, his hands trembling uncontrollably on the bar. "Two double whiskeys. Bourbon. And what do you want?" he asked, turning to Tina.

But Tina had her eyes on the bartender. "Why are you shaking your head?" she asked him.

"'Cause I ain't giving him no more whiskey, that's why," said Toby.

Matt was immediately outraged. "What!" he roared. He stood up from his stool in a hurry, sending it tumbling down to the floor behind him.

"Just calm your ass down," Toby said, not threatened. "I'll give you a beer if you want beer. No more whiskey."

"Why?" asked Matt, now sounding more like a sulky schoolboy.

"Because you got that crazy look in your eye, all right? You get all fired up and upset and no one can stop you. You're too big and wild. Last time you broke five bottles from behind the bar and a bunch of glasses. And you never paid me for it. Well I ain't dealing with it. Not today."

"All right, fine," Matt said, reaching into his pocket and pulling out a ten dollar bill. He held it out for Toby to take. "I'm sorry about the fucking glasses, if that's what this is all about. Now give me my fucking whiskey, will you?"

Toby snatched the bill out from his fingers. "I appreciate that. But I still ain't getting you any whiskey."

Now it was go-time. "What! Fuck you, old man! Nobody cuts me off! I can drink anyone in here under the bar! Let's go! I'll prove it! Who wants it? Who wants a piece of this? Huh?" Matt called out, screaming now so that everyone in the bar could hear him.

This tirade brought relative silence to the bar before he was answered by the cool, even voice of the man seated to his left.

"You know what?" asked Jack, spinning around in his stool to face Matt.

"What?" Matt asked, cautiously.

"Why don't you sit down and shut the fuck up? You're starting to piss me off, too," Jack snarled at him. He let Matt look at him full in the face for a moment, showing him his dark scruff and his dead, coal-black eyes. There was nothing in there. Nothing. He spun back around to face the bar, cigarette smoke emanating from him as if it was seeping out of every orifice in his head.

Matt stood still and felt all the eyes on him. *Now* what the hell was he supposed to do? Coming from anyone else that would have meant nothing to him, but from Jack it was a different story. To say that Jack and he were *friends* would be a bit of an overstatement. They spoke, which is more than most people could say when it came to Jack. But Jack didn't *like* anybody. For some unknown reason he could tolerate Matt to a certain extent, and for this he was more of a friend to him than anyone else in camp was.

Matt had good reason to be wary of Jack. While lots of guys carried guns out there, Jack was the only guy he'd actually seen use one. Just the other week he watched him gun down a Grizzly bear. The bear was headed away from camp and Jack had just spotted him off in the distance, through the soft rain. They tracked him down and Jack shot him, first at long range in the back of the head and then up close in the head over and over and over again. Jack had said that it was too close to camp; that they couldn't afford to take the chance of having a monster like that prowling around. But Matt saw that it was something else. For a moment, just after he was done blasting, he saw something come to life in Jack's black eyes for the first time. It was something he did not wish to see again.

Jack confessed to Matt that he had escaped from prison, where he was serving a life sentence for killing a man. This place, out in the logging camp away from civilization, was as far away as he could run. He said it was probably only a matter of time before he killed somebody else. He liked it. And he told Matt he'd be happy to make *him* that special somebody if he told anybody about him bouncing from prison.

So Matt stood there in The Gearbox, grinding his teeth and clenching his fists, wondering what he could possibly do now to save face. Maybe he could pick up his fallen stool, fling it out the door, and then follow it out. Yeah, that could work. He bent over, gripped the bottom legs of the stool and prepared to wing it behind him when he was interrupted.

"No! Matt, wait!" called Tina, springing to his rescue.

God bless her, Matt thought. He let go of the stool and straightened up to meet her. "What is it?" he demanded harshly, playing out the part.

Tina stepped close and put her fingers on his chest. "Who needs 'em?" she whispered in his ear. "I have plenty of booze at my place. Let's go. I'm ready for you, anyway."

Matt smiled at her, grabbed hold of her hand, and the two of them left the bar without saying another word.

Outside, the bright afternoon sunlight made them both flinch and shade their eyes. Tina's candy apple red Camaro was parked in the dirt parking lot, nearly glowing in the midst of a dozen beat-up pickup trucks. The two of them giggled on their way to the car, and Tina leaned into him as much for support as from desire.

"Gimme the keys," said Matt.

"No way," answered Tina. "You've had way more to drink than me."

"That may be true. But look at you. Who can walk the straighter line?"

Matt left her side, being careful to steady her upright before he let her go, and walked an imaginary line in the dirt. While it wasn't the straightest line in the world, he did hop confidently on one foot at the very end for effect.

Tina tossed the keys in the air and Matt snatched them without even having to look for them.

"Just be careful," she said.

"Of course," Matt answered, grinning, already picturing the white lines zipping by while he pinned the pedal to the floor.

They got in the car and Matt felt the smoothness of the black leather seats underneath his jeans. He put in the clutch and turned the key, churning the engine to life. It roared, more from a leaky exhaust than a finely tuned engine, but it sounded beautiful to Matt nonetheless.

"Oh, yeah! Purring, baby, purring!" he announced, delighted.

"It's all right. Let's do some more blow before we drive," she said. "I think it makes me drive better, more focused, when I'm buzzing."

"Me too," Matt lied.

"Makes me horny, too," said Tina, giggling.

Tina went through her purse and laid out a couple lines on a little vanity mirror. There was a rolled dollar bill all set up from prior usage. She held it out to Matt for the first whack; a truly courteous lady.

Matt leaned in and sucked back the line hungrily. As it burned him up he mashed down on the gas and let the engine rip, with the clutch still pressed to the floor. And before Tina could even treat herself, he let it out in reverse.

"Yeah-heah!" he bellowed, ripping backwards through the parking lot at thirty miles an hour, all in a cloud of dirt and flying gravel.

"Whoa! Stop it! Stop it you asshole!" Tina screamed.

Matt mashed the brakes and jerked the wheel hard, sending the car fishtailing in between two parked pickup trucks, faced out at the open road. He looked over at Tina for a split second, her face sober with horror, before grinning and juicing it forward in first gear. Dust and small rocks peppered the trucks behind them, and the tires squealed when they jumped from the dirt of the parking lot onto the asphalt of the two-lane highway.

"Stop it! Please! Stop it!" Tina pleaded.

Matt had set out with the intention of cooling it for a while after he got out on the highway, but something about seeing Tina begging him to stop made him want to take it further.

"What? Are you scared?" he asked, whipping hard through second and third gears in the matter of seconds.

"Yes! Please!" Tina shrieked, and then her voice became barely audible. "Please," she whimpered.

"You think I can't drive? I grew up racing cars," he lied again. He raced through fourth gear and threw it into fifth, and dropped a steel-toed boot down on the gas. There was no one else on the road. It was wide open, a dream come true. Matt shifted his glance between the road and the speedometer. 90... 100... 105... 110... 112. 112? That's it? It had to have more than that.

He didn't see the stop sign coming until it was too late. Matt pulled his foot off the gas for a split second while he figured it. Going that fast, there was no way to stop in time. Might as well punch it straight through.

"Hold on!" he roared, and floored it again.

Tina had been huddled against the door, resigned to death. But now she allowed curiosity to get the best of her. She opened her eyes just in time to see the four-way stop sign and the Oregon State Trooper inching forward off the stop and then stopping just shy of the exact middle of the intersection.

Matt kept his foot firmly on the gas, smiled, and moved the wheel a mere centimeter to his left. The Camaro whizzed by the front bumper of the squad car, clearing it by less than a foot and leaving it shaking back and forth from the velocity.

Matt saw the red and blue lights flip on and the trooper wrench the wheel to come after him. He was loving it now, in full-on laughter.

"See?" he announced. "It's fine. He'll never catch us. Didn't even get our plate, we were moving so fast."

But Tina didn't think it was fine. She looked over at him in tears, her cheeks black and blue from her running mascara. "Matt! Please just pull over! You're going to kill us both! I know it!" She managed to blurt out amidst chokes and sobs.

Matt recognized in her face that his chances of getting laid that afternoon had taken a serious nose-dive. He felt a small hint of regret at everything that had happened in the past few minutes, and even considered that some of it might have been his own fault. Then it all turned to anger. The bile boiled inside his throat and he searched for someone to blame.

Toby! That fucker! If he hadn't cut him off, none of this would have ever happened!

Matt jammed on the brakes and cut the wheel, sending the Camaro in an about-face of burning rubber and smoke.

Tina opened the door and tried to jump out, but Matt was quick.

"Oh, no you don't!" he scolded her, grabbing her arm and jerking her back towards him.

He reached across and pulled the partially opened door closed. Then he hit the gas again and raced through the gears, speeding directly at the State Trooper. The cop was wisely not in the mood for a game of chicken. He pulled way off the road onto the grassy brush, allowing Matt to whiz by. Then he quickly, but under control, wheeled around back in pursuit.

Matt figured he had a couple minutes on him. That was all he needed. He gunned it right back through the four-way stop, leaving the aluminum signs shaking in his wake, and motored down the homestretch back to The

Gearbox. When he got there he skidded to a stop out front, starting on the asphalt and ending up in the dirt of the parking lot right behind Jack's beat up old Dodge pickup. The truck had no tailgate. He saw his chain saw with the four-foot bar in the back of the bed, gleaming in the sunlight. It was like it was calling out to him. That's what he would do, then.

"Better get out now," he warned Tina.

Tina didn't hesitate. She opened the door and started running, not into the bar but straight across the open field in hysteria.

Matt jumped out and walked over to the saw. The rage was boiling in him, and everything he looked at seemed to have a coating of red haze over it. He could hear the siren getting closer in the distance. He'd better hurry up.

He grabbed onto the saw and pulled the choke out. He ripped at the starter once and then again; nothing. *Dammit!* He shuddered. *Not now!*

And with the next mighty rip of the starter the saw coughed to life. He revved it high right away, with the throttle all the way down, and kept it that way as he started walking. The hum of the motor changed in pitch once he got indoors. Men scattered away from him in all directions as he stormed up to the bar. At last he let his finger off the throttle trigger.

"You want to cut me off, do you?" Matt roared.

Toby had run to the far end of the bar, as far away as he could get without hurdling over it. "What are you doing?" he managed to get out, hoarsely.

"You want to cut me off? Then this is what you get, you old fuck!"

Matt revved up the throttle to full bore again. He raised the saw up above the bar and brought it down and through the wood slowly and expertly, as if he were making a precision pressure cut on a fallen limb. The chain ate through the three-inch-thick bar cleanly, leaving a smooth cut and a pile of sawdust on the floor.

Matt let his finger off the throttle and took a moment to admire his work.

"Drop the saw!" came an angry voice from behind him.

He heard the click of greased metal-on-metal and turned to see the tall State Trooper in his dark brown uniform, leveling his pistol right at his chest.

"Whoa! Take it easy!" said Matt.

"Drop the saw!" repeated the trooper.

"Fine. It's nothing. Just a little misunderstanding," Matt said. He flipped the OFF switch and laid his hot saw down on the plank wood floor.

"Toby'll tell you," Matt explained.

"Get this... crazy sonofabitch... out of here," Toby stammered.

The trooper took a step closer. "I'm going to put these cuffs on you. Are you going to let me, or no? Do you want to resist arrest, too?"

"Hell no," Matt said, holding his arms out. "Although I really don't think it's necessary. I'm not gonna do anything. I was just having a little fun with my friend Toby here. We're buddies. Aren't we?"

"Turn around," said the trooper. He spun Matt around and put the cuffs on him behind his back. Then he slammed the side of his face down on the bar, right next to his fresh cut. It smelled awful, like burning lacquer. "You're in big trouble, boy. You trying to kill me, driving like that?"

"*Driving?*" Matt repeated, and chuckled. "I don't know what you're talking about. I haven't driven in years. Don't even have my license."

As Matt finished speaking he caught a glimpse of Jack looking down at him from the other end of the bar. He was calmly smoking a cigarette, and hadn't budged from his barstool throughout the whole thing. He was the only one seated at the bar. And he looked down at Matt smiling, showing his rotten teeth, his eyes twinkling like they did with the bear.

CHAPTER 8

We were all sitting on Matt's couch in the morning, waiting for the plan. It was Tim, Weeman and I. The first couple days I worked for him, I was shocked by the way he had us just sitting there while he made phone calls and yakkity-yakked with us about nothing for an hour while we were on the clock. It would have made any other boss sick, thinking about the money he was wasting. Matt could care less.

Finally Tim spoke up. He must have been getting bored with the TV and felt his belly sufficiently filled with coffee.

"What's the hold up, Mickey?" he asked, his arms crossed and his head nestled back into the corner of the couch. His eyes were half-open. "I thought we had that big job over in Portsmouth you were talking about. What happened? You didn't get the green light?"

Matt was shuffling through a hundred random sheets of perforated computer paper that were piled on his kitchen table. He scribbled notes on them and then lost track of where he put them. They were all over the house.

His mornings were an endless cycle of shuffling through them, thinking he found what he was looking for, and then continuing the search.

"No," he said absently, focused on his papers.

"You've gone and mucked it up, haven't you?" asked Weeman.

"You shut up, Weeman!" said Matt, raising his voice. I looked up, half-awake myself, and expected to see him red in the face with anger. Instead he was smiling. He pounded his coffee mug down on the table for added effect. "Don't speak unless you're spoken to!"

"You blew it, Mickey! You loser! I knew it!" said Weeman.

"I didn't blow it. I decided not to do it. I'm gonna save it… the trees," he said, and resumed his search among the papers. "It's too important… to big… to cut. You wouldn't understand, Weeman. All you care about is yourself. And booze. And Jan-Jan."

Jan-Jan was Weeman's girlfriend, although that's not how he described their relationship to me. He told me he was her sex-slave. She was forty, Puerto-Rican, and married to a man who had alleged ties to the Italian mob in Providence. Weeman told me he sometimes feared for his life when he laid in bed at night, but that saga is another story altogether.

"You're an idiot, Mickey. It's the middle of winter. You should take what you can get. Look at us, sitting around on your fucking couch. You don't even have any work, do you?"

"Fuck you, Weeman! Don't talk to me anymore or your fired!" he yelled, and laughed. Arguing with Weeman was the most fun he had all day, right up until the point where both of them got genuinely upset. Then they would keep their distance from each other until the next morning. "I got plenty of work," he continued. "Tim, you take Weeman and go over to the gay mansion."

"The gay mansion? Really?" Tim asked, his face brightening.

"Yeah. Matthew Large-ge-hess. Matthew Large-ge-hess," Matt bellowed in a gay falsetto, sing-song voice. He chuckled, and then his face turned serious without transition. "Me and Shame are going to Connecticut to see Eleanor. We have to go… look at a job. Just do the pruning we do every year, there. You know the program, right?"

"Yeah," said Tim, hesitantly. "Why are you taking him if you just have to look at a job? Can't you leave him with us? We could probably use him to help clean up over there."

"No. Shame comes with me. Right?" he asked me.

"Sure," I said. "Whatever's best for the team." It was a cold, windy morning and the thought of a nice, warm, long truck ride sounded awful good to me.

"Good," said Matt. "I have to talk to this lady and it'd be good to have you there. People like you. I don't know why."

I laughed. "I don't know why, either."

"No. You're a good kid. I mean… you just have something about you. It makes people like you, *I* think."

"Thanks," I said.

Tim stood up, stretched his arms behind his back and got one last good yawn in. "Well… good luck buddy," he said, slapping me on the back. "Have a fun ride. It's a long one, you know. Over an hour, both ways. A lot of talking time. You want a dip for the road?"

I had quickly climbed to the top of Tim's graces for the simple fact that I was willing to partake in some chew with him at times. "Nah," I said. "Too early in the morning for me."

"Suit yourself. Come on, Dom," Tim said to Weeman.

Weeman stood up to his full five-foot stature and leveled a forefinger at Matt as he walked out. "You're stupid, Mickey. You should have taken that job. Mark my words. The operation's going belly-up. Truly, you're an idiot."

"Get out of my house!" Matt roared, grinning. "And don't come back tomorrow! I mean it! I don't want to see you here tomorrow! You're fired!"

❧

We got to Eleanor Higgins' house at about 11 am. For as much as Tim and Weeman complained about Matt's company, you would think that an hour-long truck ride with the guy was a form of torture. I, myself, always had a pretty good time with him. I made kind of a game out of it. It sounds mean, like I was picking on him, but I really wasn't. He seemed to enjoy it; at least he never let on otherwise. I found out how to press his buttons over time, and when I really had a feel for it I could control his emotions like I was at the operating panel of some kind of humanoid robot. When I sensed him getting fired up, I could say something that I knew would send him off steaming. Then I could let him tear on until I'd had enough and say the right things to calm him down again. And I had a secret weapon for when it all got too weird. We had a common bond, something that could eat up hours on end if necessary. We could talk Celtics basketball. So whenever he got jumpy on me, I went straight to hoops talk and our minds could both be operating on the same plane.

Eleanor's house was a big, white colonial affair built high on top of a rock formation in the woods of eastern Connecticut, just over the Rhode Island border. As we rolled up onto the long paved driveway and I saw that big old house sitting up there, my first impression was that the place was haunted. There was very little lawn, if any, surrounding the house and it gave the impression that it had simply risen out of the trees and rocks. Even the weathered wooden shingles blended in with the dull gray color of the winter skyline.

We settled to a stop in front of the two-car garage. We were situated well below the front entrance; there was a steep stone path that led from the parking area up to the house. Matt cut the engine and stared straight ahead into the blankness of the newly painted white garage doors. And he sat there like that for a good five seconds. It was longest I'd ever witnessed him go without talking, so I figured he must be a little nervous.

He let me in on his plan on the ride over. This lady was one of his wealthiest clients. She was also someone who cared deeply about the environment. She had been involved with preservation projects in the past, more than just by contributing money. She helped raise funds and had been key in the developmental stages of getting some small parcels of land set aside for neighborhood parks in New York. Matt wanted to get her interested in Oakland Forest. He saw this as his only real shot. He figured if he couldn't get her support, it would be nearly impossible.

"Are you nervous?" I asked.

"No," he said quickly, and I could tell he was lying.

"Don't worry about it," I told him. "You got this. It's like you said: it's not like you're going up there, asking for money. You're just here to let her know what's going on, and to ask her for some advice about how to save it. That'll be enough to get her to bite, if she's into it."

"Yeah," Matt answered, sullenly.

I laughed. "What the hell are you worried about? You're a charmer. You said this lady likes you, right?"

"*Loves* me," he said, correcting me.

"See? So what's the problem?"

"Okay. Let's go," he said. And with that he was off, out the door and storming up the path for the front door.

He always did this to me. No matter how ready I thought I was, he had twenty paces on me by the time I got out of the truck. "Hey!" I called after him. "You want me to gas up the saws? Get the ropes ready or something?"

"No," he said, sounding annoyed. He kept moving and barked back over his shoulder, "Let's go! I need you. Come on!"

The guy was genuinely angry with me, just like that. What a lunatic! I laughed to myself as I jogged up the walkway to catch up with him, and got there just as he rang the doorbell.

"Mmm-hmm! Mmm-hmm," Matt said to himself while we were waiting. I looked away and down at the gardens so he wouldn't see me laughing at him. It got worse after we heard footsteps coming to the door. "Mmm-hmm! Mmm-hmm! Mmm-hmm!" It took all I had to hold it together.

The woman who opened up the door looked like an angel. She had soft, pale, smooth skin and a kind expression on her face, even though she wasn't exactly smiling. It was something within her. She had long blonde hair that was fading to white and she let it hang off to the sides of her cheekbones, only partially tucked behind her ears. The soft white light from behind her in the foyer played off her hair, making it seem like she was glowing.

"Oh, hi Eleanor! Hi!" Matt started, all in a ball of fire. "How's it going? Yeah! Great! Great that you could meet me. Thanks. How are you?"

"I'm fine, Matthew. And how are you?"

"Good. Great. Hey, the reason I wanted to talk to you is because I found this forest in Portsmouth, Rhode Island. The developers called me to give them a price to clear the place, but I don't want to do it. I don't want anyone to do it. There's beech trees there that I think are old growth. Even if they're not, it's a special place. It's like… magic. I can feel it. Anyway, I wanted to get your advice on how to save it because I know you've done stuff like this before."

Eleanor's face had grown stranger and more distant while Matt was talking. Now it almost seemed like she was afraid of him.

"Oh," Matt said. "Is this a bad time or something? I'm sorry if—"

"No… no," said Eleanor. "It's nothing like that. It's…"

Here she paused and looked at me, confused.

"Hi," I said. "I'm Shamus Flaherty. I work with Matt. I'm a writer. I'm going to help him with the forest… you know… if we need to write stuff down," I told her, creating an excuse for my presence.

"Oh, hi Shamus," she said. "Nice to meet you." And then to Matt, "No. Forgive me. I'm just a little taken aback. I… well… I don't know how to tell you this. It's going to sound as strange to you as it did to me."

"Why? What's the matter?" Matt asked.

"Nothing's wrong. It's just… well… I got a very strange phone call this morning that now seems even stranger."

"A phone call?" Matt repeated.

"Yes. It was a woman named Crystal Powers. She calls herself a futurist. Other people call her a fortune teller, or a witch. Do you know what she told me?"

"What?"

"She told me you were coming here today to ask me for my help in saving a forest, and that it was a very special place of ancient importance. She told me to tell you that she needs to meet with you, today, to talk with you about it. She wants to meet you at the Chinese restaurant in town. It's urgent. She repeated that word often, *urgent*."

I felt the chills come over me when she was talking, so strong that I had to look away. By the way Matt was looking I could tell he was feeling it too.

"Come on," said Matt, breaking into a smile. "What are you doing to me?"

Eleanor shook her head negatively to imply that she wasn't kidding. "And there's more," she said, smiling. Her face lit up when she smiled, enough to chase the chills away from me.

Both Matt and I stood there, smiling back at her dumbly.

"Rumor has it that she hasn't left her condominium in ten years. And now, today, she wants to go out and have lunch with *you*. At a Chinese restaurant."

"Wow," said Matt.

"Yes. I'm supposed to call her to confirm as soon as you get here. So, will you be meeting her?"

Eleanor was smiling, enjoying watching Matt squirm while he tried to make sense of all this. Knowing Matt, I assumed it was because Matt had often left her scratching her head with some of the stunts he'd pulled in the past, and now this was her revenge.

"I don't know," Matt said. "All that stuff… that fortune telling stuff… it all seems kind of weird, doesn't it? I mean… I don't know. Does it?"

"It is strange," Eleanor agreed. "But she's been so dead-on with everything she said. I would go and talk to her. Just talk to her. What's the harm in that?"

"I don't know," Matt said. "Just seems kind of weird."

"Put it this way, Matthew," said Eleanor. "I am so intrigued by this whole thing that I need to know what she tells you. Go there and talk to her, and I promise to help you with the forest. Okay?"

The Chinese restaurant, The Golden Dragon, was in the middle of a small strip mall, tucked in between a franchised barbershop and a liquor store.

"This old bat hasn't left her house in ten years, and *this* is where she wants to go?" I asked, sitting in the truck with Matt.

"How do you know she's an old bat?" he asked.

"I'm just assuming. You heard Eleanor. She said some people call her a witch. Witches are old bats."

"You really think she's a witch?" he asked, with a glint of true fear behind his pale blue eyes.

"Could be," I said, laying it on. "I believe in that stuff. Witches, ghosts... all that. I believe our spirits are carried on somehow after we're gone, be it through mere memories or even manifested in some corporeal form." I looked out my window so he couldn't see me trying to hide my grin. I wasn't sure if I'd used *corporeal* correctly.

"What the hell?" he exclaimed, cursing his situation. "You're coming in there with me, right?"

"Absolutely not," I told him, turning back to him and showing him I was laughing.

"Come on!"

"No way. She wants *you*. She doesn't even know about me. And that's the way I want to keep it. Let me let you in on a little rule I have: if there's a choice between meeting a witch and not meeting a witch, I don't meet her."

"I don't care about rules. You have to come. I'm the boss, and you'll do what I tell you or you don't get paid," he said, dead serious.

"Sorry, Matt. We just passed a little bar that looked like they had burgers in there. I'm gonna go sit down, have a beer and a burger, and I'll meet you back at the truck in half an hour."

I got out of the truck and started walking.

"Get back here. You wimp! You're a pussy!" he called after me.

I looked back to see his head propped over the cab of the truck. He was standing on the floorboards; his head was the only thing I could see. And he was not happy. There was a little white foam forming at the corner of his mouth.

"Words don't bother me, man," I hollered back, and kept walking.

❧

I came walking back to the truck, my belly nice and greased down from a half-pound cheeseburger, to find Matt sitting behind the wheel with the engine running. He was staring out the window with a glazed look in his eyes, and he didn't even flinch when I got into the truck and sat next to him. He was brooding, with his black winter skull-cap pulled down low to his eyebrows. He looked like a trauma victim.

"How was lunch?" I asked.

"I didn't eat," he said.

"Why not?"

"I couldn't."

"What happened? She put a belly curse on you?" I asked, twinkling my fingers and smiling at him.

He turned to face me for the first time. "You're a real pussy, you know that?"

"Call me what you will," I said.

He looked back out his window. "That was the craziest thing I've ever seen. And I've done a lot of crazy shit. I told you. I used to do drugs… everything… I'd smoke anything that burned. I lived at Kesey's ranch for a month. Nothing like this."

"Kesey? You mean Ken Kesey? You met him?" I asked.

"You know what she told me?" he asked, ignoring my question.

"What?"

"She told me she's seen me before in visions… in dreams. She knew who I was right when I walked in. 'Matthew! Matthew! Over here!' she said. I've never met her before in my life and she knew who I was. She was like… overjoyed to see me. She gave me a big hug right there in the restaurant. She like… got down on her knees she was so happy. Everyone was looking at us. She's dressed up like some kind of Buddhist monk or something. Flowing robe."

"Yeah?"

"She said she recognized my face perfectly from visions. She said I was the one. The *chosen* one. She said I've been chosen to be the voice of the forest. That I need to speak for the trees because they can't speak for themselves. But they will speak to me, and I'll be able to hear them. She said I will save the forest, that it's going to be hard and it's going to look like it's not going to happen but it will. She said Oakland Forest is a very special place, that it's got healing powers like that place in France. Chamoneiux… or Chateau Blue… or something like that. You know what I'm talking about?" he asked, and turned to face me.

"Not really," I confessed.

He made a face to show me his disgust in my ignorance, then continued, staring hard at me as if he were accusing me of something. "She said angels will rise out of the forest floor in celebration when the forest is finally saved, and that I will see them. *And* she said that this is just the beginning for me. That this is going to change my whole life; that I will continue to be the voice of the forest after this. And that I'm going to save more places. You believe that?"

"That's pretty crazy," I admitted.

"But do you believe it?"

"I don't know," I answered, hoping that would be good enough. But it wasn't. Matt was still staring at me, waiting for an answer. "I really don't know," I said. "It'd definitely freak me out if it happened to me, though."

"Yeah," he said, and sighed.

"But it doesn't really matter what I think. How do *you* feel about it? Do *you* think it could be true?"

"I kind of do," Matt said, looking serious enough. "I feel like it's all true, like she was telling me stuff that I kind of already knew, but didn't. It's weird."

"Yeah. Crazy," I said.

Matt suddenly perked up in his seat. "Here she is!" he said.

There was a ghostly woman coming out of the restaurant, walking into the parking lot. Her long white silky robe was sailing around her in the breeze.

"Oh, shit," I said. "She's still here?"

"That's her!" Matt said, and then he remembered my fear. "You're gonna meet her, you pussy!"

"No! No. That's all right," I said.

"Hey! Hey Crystal!" he called out the window. "Come on over here!"

"Whoa! What are you doing, dude?" I asked him.

Now he was giggling. "Yeah. See how *you* like it."

She waved and began walking at us. I studied her while she stepped off the curb and walked through the parking lot. If there were such things as witches, she was definitely one of them. She was pale as the new fallen snow, a stark contrast to the piles of dirty plowed ice in the corners of the parking lot. All of her being was so white, she appeared to be glowing. Her hair, her skin... everything was the same true white as her silken robe. The hem of the robe dragged along the dirty pavement, and I could see her pale bare feet poking out from underneath at each stride.

"Holy shit," I said.

"Yeah. What's the matter, you scared? Shame! Shame! Come on! Here's your big chance!" he taunted.

When she got close to the truck, I pretended like I was searching for something on the floor by my feet. I figured it'd be best if I didn't make eye contact.

"Hey! I just wanted to say sorry I didn't stay and eat. I was a little freaked out, but I appreciate it... all the stuff you said."

"Oh, it's fine," said Crystal. Her voice was high, soft and sweet. "People react like that often when I tell them things."

"Yeah. Hey, I want you to meet my buddy, Shamus Flaherty."

Now I had to look up. And when I did I found something that wasn't white on her. She had emerald green eyes. I gulped. "Hi," I offered.

"I have not seen you," she said in a matter-of-fact way. "But your presence is familiar."

"Thank you," I replied, and was startled by the gargled sound of my own voice. The fear was constricting my vocal cords, the way I had only felt before in dreams.

"Yeah!" Matt roared. "Shame's a writer. He lives right by me, in Jamestown. He's a famous writer. He's gonna write a book about me saving the forest."

"Is that so?" Crystal asked.

"No," I said. "That's a complete lie. He lies, sometimes. I'm just a tree worker. I'm helping Matt with the tree thing."

"But you are a writer," said Crystal, and scrutinized me for another moment. "And a musician," she finished.

I looked down at my feet again and played with the empty coffee cups on the floor.

"Yup!" Matt chimed in. "He's a rock star. He has rock star night every Thursday, comes in smelling like booze on Friday. Isn't that right, Shame? What's the matter? What are you looking for down there?"

"Oh, Matthew," said Crystal, straightening her robe with a flourish. "I forgot to mention—I'll be sending you blessings as this affair proceeds."

"Blessings?"

"Blessings. They'll be in paper-form. They are essential. Without them, it will not be possible. You'll need to bring them to the forest and tuck them under the leaf-litter on the forest floor. This is how they will be received."

"Received... by who?" Matt asked.

"By the forest," Crystal said, with her same matter-of-fact tone. "By the spirits within. I have to go, now. I don't like being out here in the real world. I am flooded by so much... it's overwhelming. Good-bye," she said. And then she added over her shoulder, "I have your address."

We watched her walk through the parking lot, out towards the main road.

"Hey!" Matt bellowed after her. "Don't you want a ride or something?"

"Are you fucking nuts?" I whispered.

As she turned towards us the wind picked up and whipped her white hair and her robe wildly all about her, covering her face. "I prefer to walk, thank you," she called back.

We watched her walk away, leaning forward into the wind, with her robe and hair flying and her bare pale feet plodding along the dirty asphalt, looking like she may be blown into flight with the next strong gust.

CHAPTER 9

(back for the last time)

It was in the basement of St. Mark's Church in Providence where Matt attended his first Alcoholics Anonymous meeting. He took the drive to Providence, figuring that his problems were too far out-there for a small town meeting. The big city was bound to have more people as twisted as he was. St. Mark's basement was a depressing enough place on its own, with its faded green and tan asbestos floor tiles and dark-stained brown paneling on the walls and ceilings. The only natural light limped in through the narrow windows up high on the walls, even with ground level outside. It was in the evening in late summer and the dim orange glow of the setting sun was about to give way completely to the lines of florescent lights hanging from the ceiling. Add to the ambiance the sordid autobiographic tales of how all these miserable people ruined their lives, and it was about all Matt could do to keep from breaking down and weeping.

He was vaguely listening to the woman next to him ramble on about how she drank day and night until she couldn't hold her job, had her three-year-old daughter taken away from her, and started banging guys for booze money until she got the clap. He wondered what good this could do, and was considering walking out just as he was spoken to by the master of ceremonies for the evening.

"Well. I see we have a new guest here tonight," said the man, an old gray-haired veteran who looked like he had been run over by a train or two in his lifetime. He was a skinny guy with a red nose and bags under his eyes. He was dressed like a carpenter; wearing boots, jeans and a red flannel shirt. All the chairs were aligned in a circle, with the MC seated at about three o'clock from where Matt was. He had his legs folded and his arms crossed and an air of complete resignation.

"Mmm-hmm," Matt began. "Oh... me? Am I the only new guy? Really?"

"You are," said the MC. "I'm sorry we didn't get you in right away, but Cheryl got cut-off last week at the end of our session, and it's very important to hear everyone out all the way. It's the only way to get it out. It's also very important to us to make everyone who comes in here feel welcome. You *are* welcome here. This will be your support group. Everyone here is like a brother or sister to you in your fight for sobriety. Why don't you introduce yourself, say how long you've been sober for, and tell us a little bit about why you're here."

"Mmm-hmm! Okay," Matt said, standing up out of his aluminum folding chair. He hooked his thumbs on the bib of his overall chaps and cleared his throat. "Well... my name's Matt and I—"

"Hi, Matt," the group of ten or twelve droned.

"Wow," said Matt. "You guys really do that?"

His audience responded with silence, so he proceeded, staring straight ahead at the pile of folded tables and chairs in the corner of the room.

"I'm Matt. And I'm not really sober now, but I'd like to be. I mean... I'm not drunk right now or anything... I haven't had a drop all day. But I was drinking, *heavy,* two nights ago. I must have put down most of a bottle of Jack Daniels. I don't know. When I drink, I just feel like I have to keep drinking and I do it until I black out and don't remember stopping. When I stop, it's just an accident, really. Maybe I get so drunk that I lose my bottle, or can't get up off the ground to get it."

His audience purred with recognition.

"And you're here because you want to stop?" asked the MC.

Matt took a deep breath. "Yes," he said. He had his floppy, fisherman's style sun hat clenched in his hands, and began twisting it between his fingers. His wild eyes watered up, and a few tears escaped down his cheeks. It felt so foreign to him that it took him a moment to realize what was happening. It was the first time he could remember crying while he was sober in at least five years. Matt choked it back hard to keep the floodgates from opening, and began with a shaky voice.

"I want to quit. But I don't know if I can. I don't even *think* I can. Because there's something wrong with me. I'm not... normal. I don't know if anything can fix me."

"Matt," said the MC compassionately. "That's not *you.* That's the alcohol talking. Right now, you're the weakened man that booze has brought you to be. It makes you feel powerless, like you don't have a choice in the matter. You'll see that the longer you can remain sober, the more power you'll build up. And eventually, you'll know that you don't ever want another drink ever again."

"That sounds good," Matt said. He wiped the tears off his cheeks and started in again with a strong voice. "But I'm not sure if it'll work like that with me."

"Why not?"

"Because. I'm telling you… there's something wrong with me. I have problems. I'm not like other people. I'm like an alien or something. I have problems with… everything. Everything that's bad for you, I have a problem with. I told you about the booze, but there's other things too. Like drugs. I'm better with that now, but if somebody has something and they're willing to share then I'll do it all night until its gone. I don't care what it is. And if I can get more, then I'll buy more so we can keep going. Sex. Sex! I'm like a sex addict. I'll fuck anybody and anything I can get into. No guys, though. That's gross. But you know what I mean. I'll do the ugliest girl like… just so I can do it. I'll pay for it. I'll jerk-off ten times in one afternoon. And… gambling. Same thing. I'll gamble until all my money's gone… I've gotten into debt and thought people were going to kill me, and then I'll do it again. I've lost all my money, *everything,* like five times in my life. You understand what I'm saying? It's like I have no control over anything. It's like… it's not even like I like any of this shit that much. It's my personality. It won't let me stop. When I do something,

I just go crazy with it and keep doing it and doing it until it's not normal and something bad happens."

Here Matt caught himself and remembered there was an audience around him. He looked around at a few of their faces, and felt ashamed. "Mmm-hmm. Mmm-hmm! I'm not sure I should have said all that—I just have to talk about it with somebody. That's what this place is for, right?"

"That's exactly what this place is for," said the MC. "And there's no need to be embarrassed or anything. You did great. Your story is similar to most of the people's in here. You'll see. You're going to find out that you're not some kind of freak. Well... we are kind of freaks," he said.

The small gathering chuckled.

"But that's just what the alcohol has turned us into. We're all alike, here. Each one of us lived their own personal horror movie. You'll see that as you grow in your sobriety, you'll gain back the control over your life."

"Mmmhmm," Matt said, skeptically. "But what about all the other shit. The sex... and the drugs."

"There *are* other support groups that deal with those things, individually. There's Narcotics Anonymous for drug abuse and there's a group that meets for sex addiction, too. But you may find that once you stop drinking and the control builds up, these other things are just problems that stem from the drinking. In other words, if you're not completely possessed by the alcohol in the first place, you may not even be interested in the drugs or the sex."

"Mmmhmm," Matt echoed. "I'll tell you, I don't think so. I love sex. And drugs… it's kind of just like booze to me. I don't particularly love them but I'll just do them both the same."

"Well, there's no reason why you can't go to these other meetings, too. In fact, some people find the need to go to a meeting every night of the week in the beginning. It makes it easier."

"I still do," chimed in a man in a suit from across the circle. He was clean-cut and looked like a banker or a lawyer or something, someone who Matt wouldn't suspect to have a problem. "And I've been sober almost a year," he continued.

"There you have it," said the MC.

"Mmmhmm. You guys really think you can help me, huh? You really think I have a shot at this?"

The members of the circle nodded in confirmation.

"I *know* we can help you. And I know you can do this, if you want it bad enough."

"Mmm-hmm! Well… I better clear my calendar," Matt said with a grin. "I got a lot of meetings to go to!"

CHAPTER 10

I was down on the ground running the saw, cutting up downed pieces of brush and limb-wood so we could throw it in the chipper. A big old Norway Maple had snapped in a windstorm and did just about as much damage as one tree could do. The tree was growing right on the property line between two homes, shooting up over a stockade fence. When it snapped and crashed, it crumpled the fence, took out a portion of the roof over the garage, and ultimately landed on the little Honda parked in the driveway. The roof of the car was crumpled halfway down to the level of the doors under the weight of the wood, and all the windows were smashed out. There was glass everywhere, pieces of jagged wood and nails sticking out, all anxious to get a piece of me.

It was one of the rare cases where I had the toughest job out of all of us. Tim was harnessed into a tree right next to the broken one, dangling there, working his way down and sawing big chunks off the main trunk. Weeman was dragging brush like an animal, as usual. The bulk of the tree was resting on the ground or the car or hung up in the roof or the fence, all under pressure. That meant that I had to be really careful with most of the cuts, starting on the underside of the wood and cutting slowly so I could see which way the weight was going to shift when I cut it free. I was scared, but confident. It was good to be a little scared on this job. It kept me from getting careless, and that's when guys got hurt.

It felt good to be the main man for a change. The adrenaline was pumping through me hard from the fear and I was feeling strong. It was a cold, nasty, wet day in March but with the saw running it was perfect. I had a good sweat going and I could see my breath shooting out in hot clouds. I was in decent shape from all the work, so I felt great. My wind was keeping up with me and my arms and legs weren't getting tired when I wrestled my way through the tangled limbs to get into the proper position to make the cut. The chain was nice and sharp, cutting like a dream. At that moment, there was little else I'd rather be doing with my time. I was having fun.

That is, until Matt showed up.

I saw his truck pull up and park at the bottom of the steep driveway and got a bad feeling right away. For the most part, Matt was the man when it came to tree work. But there were a few occasions when his presence only messed things up. He had a habit of showing up when we were a few hours into the job and telling us to change everything we were doing. Sometimes he was right, but the majority of the time he was wrong. Tim knew what he was doing. He set us up to get the job done safely and efficiently. It was like Matt wanted to change things just because he was the boss and wanted things done his way and his way only. It didn't matter if the way we were doing it was working or not. To change it would mean we were doing it his way and to him, his way was better.

I could tell this was going to be one he'd screw up for us. Things were going so smoothly that he could only complicate things.

I looked up at Tim and shook my head, causing my florescent orange helmet to jiggle side to side.

Tim looked down from his perch and smiled knowingly. He wore a helmet without a mesh face-mask like mine so I could make out his smile perfectly even though he was hanging twenty feet in the air. He dropped a big brown loogey, hit the throttle on the saw and continued to slice through a section of the trunk.

Matt was storming up the driveway right at me with that look in his eye, the possessed one that I hated.

"No! No! No!" he screamed at me over the noise of the saws and the chipper.

Oh great, I thought. *Here we go.* I let go of the throttle and took my saw away from the limb I was cutting. I flipped up my face-mask to deal with him.

"Not there! No! You're doing it all wrong! There! *There!*" He pointed about three feet from where I was cutting. He was looking at me like he wanted to punch me in the face. I noticed his clothes and his hard hat were nice and dry from being in the truck all morning. Our clothes were pretty much soaked through by now from the constant soft mist. Perfect.

"What?" I shouted. I had heard perfectly what he said and had even expected it, but seeing the violence behind his words put a new wrinkle in it.

"No! You're wrong! Bad! You're going to pinch the saw! You're going to get hurt! Here! Here!" He shouted, pointing.

"I've been here for two hours and haven't pinched it yet. Don't worry about it. I got it under control," I said, raising my voice over the noise.

"No! No! Here!"

"Mickey!" Tim shouted from up in the tree, his voice barely audible over all the noise. He was really giving it everything he had for us to be able to hear him. "Leave him alone, you asshole! He's doing fine! Get out of the way!"

Matt dismissed him with a wave of his hand.

"Come on! Let's go! Here!" he repeated, pointing three feet from where I was cutting.

I thought the piece I was cutting wasn't even under pressure; that I'd already freed it from where it was caught on the fence. I looked down again just to make sure. I was right. "What fucking difference does it make?" I shouted.

"You're wrong! All wrong! Here! Fuck it!"

He came at me, trying to take the saw out of me hands.

I held the saw, still idling, away from him and put my other hand on his chest to hold him away.

"Gimme it!" he shouted, reaching for it like an angry school yard bully.

"Get off me!" I yelled back at him, and stepped around to the other side of the limb. "What, you want it here?" I asked, holding the saw where he was pointing.

"Yes!"

"Fine!" I said. I made a cut up from the bottom, brought the saw back up over the limb and freed it cleanly. It hit the asphalt and Weeman dragged it away, giving Matt a cold glare on his way.

"Like it fucking matters," I said. "We're running it through the chipper! What difference does it make?" I asked.

"You don't know how to run a saw! Give it to me!" He came at me and lunged for the saw again.

This time I held the saw away and pushed him, hard, with my other hand.

My shove didn't really phase him, physically. Although he stopped coming, it wasn't from the force of my hand against his chest. He weighed about twice as much as me and was infinitely stronger. He stood perfectly still with his hands down by his sides. His face turned bright red.

"Here!" he shouted, pointing to a new limb next to us. His whole head trembled with rage, kind of like the way I saw Napoleon's head wiggle when he yelled at his troops on some re-creation battle show. Some white foam escaped from the corner of his mouth.

"What are you gonna do? Hit me?" I challenged.

"I'll hit you! I'll take your fucking head clean-off! Now cut it! Here!"

"Matt! Leave me alone! It's fine!"

"Here! Here!" He shouted maniacally.

"Say it one more time," I said.

"Here!"

I stared dead at him while I dropped the saw and let it bang against the asphalt.

"Do it yourself," I told him.

He made a rush at me, swinging his arms forward to try to get a hold of my sweatshirt. I was angry enough to fight but I wasn't stupid. To tangle with Matt was suicide. Luckily, I was a lot quicker than him. I ran back towards the base of the downed portion of the tree and left him tangled in the branches, then took off running down the driveway.

When I got halfway down the hill I turned around to see if he was still on me.

He was standing up by the mess, amidst the broken glass from the bashed car, huffing and puffing.

"You better run!" he shouted.

"Yeah? Why don't you come and get me, fat ass?"

I unbuckled my chaps (that belonged to him), keeping an eye on him to make sure he wasn't coming. He wasn't. I left the chaps laying down by my feet, turned around, and started walking.

I have to say that I felt little sense of pride, walking through the mist along the side of the road that day. In the past when I've quit jobs I've at least felt somewhat satisfied after telling somebody to shove it. I didn't feel any of that on this one. I didn't want it to end this way with Matt. He was a lunatic. I *knew* that. It wasn't necessarily his fault that he couldn't turn his OCD on and off as he pleased.

I started laughing, thinking of him repeating, "Here! Here!" with all the blood rushed up into his big fat head. And if I could laugh now, why couldn't I laugh it off five minutes ago?

It was just one of those things. I'm a stupid Mick and I get emotional. I get blinded by it, at times. And it was perfect timing. He caught me at the moment when all my stress about having a baby on the way was boiling just underneath the surface, ready to erupt. Then, enter the lunatic screaming in my face about how bad of a job I'm doing as I'm busting my ass out in the rain. It was enough to make anyone snap. I shouldn't feel so bad about it. I could find another meaningless grunt-labor job tomorrow that paid me the same amount of money or more. And that's what I was going to do. I only had a month to go before I could start up my landscaping thing. Yes, it would have been more convenient if I could have just kept this going, rather than having to find work just for a few weeks. But there was nothing I could do about that, now.

It occurred to me that I couldn't hear any noise coming from the job site anymore, so I took a look back behind me to see if there was any fallout. Just as I did, I saw Matt's little black pickup come ripping out of the driveway and out onto the road. He was juicing it towards me. The little engine was roaring.

Now I was angry again. I turned around and kept walking, this time at a steadier pace. What was he going to do now, try to flatten me with the truck? Well, if he was then I was going to let him do it. And he could rot in prison for the rest of his pathetic life.

But as the truck got near it slowed down and started rolling right behind me, even with my pace. I could hear the sand and the salt crunching underneath the tires. I wasn't even going to look. I was going to keep right on walking.

"All right, Shamus," Weeman called out in the old Scottish accent. "Would you like a ride, or do you fancy walking out in the rain all fucking day?"

I looked over to see him leaning out over the passenger side door, huffing on a cigarette. Tim was behind the wheel, grinning.

"Did I scare you?" asked Tim.

"Yeah," I admitted.

He put on the brakes. "Hop in," he said. "I'll give you a lift back to your house."

I opened the door and climbed in the tiny back seat of the extra cab. "What about Matt?" I asked.

Tim shrugged his shoulders. "I told him we were taking lunch. You know," he said, "That's happened to all of us. Everyone snaps at some point. Mickey knows he does that to people. If you go home tonight and start feeling bad about it, or whatever, you can just show up tomorrow morning. And it'll be like nothing ever happened."

"Yeah," I said. "I don't think I'm gonna do that."

CHAPTER 11

Matt pulled up in his little black pickup to find the news crew waiting for him by the entrance to the forest. There was the big white van there with the satellite dish on top, and the camera guys with all their cables and gadgets. And there was little Michelle Gonzalez, the reporter, getting her makeup done out in front of the van.

Matt twisted the key to turn off the truck and sat there giggling in delight. They were there for *him*. He couldn't believe it. He was really going to be on TV! On the ride over here, he was thinking there was no way they were really going to show up. It just seemed so impossible. *This*, this whole hullabaloo, was here for *him*. *He* was the expert authority for their report. Arborist Matthew Largess. No… Arborist Matthew "Twig" Largess. He was going to make sure they put that in there… or no story. He was big time, now. He had to start having that Forest Defenders nickname, just like Julia "Butterfly" Hill, the woman who was living in the redwood tree out west.

That was Eleanor's suggestion, the nickname thing. She was the one who really put this whole thing together. She got the Land Trust and the Nature Conservancy involved. She must have gotten the news crews involved. They were the ones that called him. He didn't have to do anything to get them to come out. And now it was *his* time to shine. He had to turn on the old charm. The snake-oil salesman had to come out and be at his best for this one. And that alone wasn't going to cut it, this time. He had to have his facts straight. He had to remember what to say.

A sudden wave of paranoia came over him. TV! What if he all of a sudden forgot everything and came off like a bumbling idiot? Or what if this reporter started asking him questions that made him look like he was lying or something? He'd seen them do that to people before. What did Eleanor say to him? She gave him a few tips. One of them was to never say anything bad about the developers. He got that. What were the others, now?

There was a rapping on his window, snapping him out of his study session.

"You the tree guy?" a man yelled through his rolled-up window. It was one of the camera guys, a bearded guy wearing a wool cap and gloves with the fingers cut off.

Matt rolled down his window and cleared his throat. "Yeah," he said. "Matthew Twig Largess."

"Great," the guy said. "Come on out and let's get things rolling. We have to get this done and get on to the next one before 4:30."

"Oh. Mmmhmm!" Matt replied. He sprang out of the truck all at once with his usual burst of speed and stood in front of the camera guy, who took a step back in wonderment of how he got there so quickly. He looked down at himself and smoothed his hands over his fleece jacket. *Looking good,* he considered. He was wearing his boots, his cleanest navy blue chaps, his maroon fleece and his black NK Sailing winter hat, pulled down low over his eyes.

"Do I look all right?" Matt asked.

"Yeah, great," the guy said, already walking. Then he looked over his shoulder and actually considered it. "Might want to take that hat off. It's up to you. Come on. Right over here."

"Oh, right," Matt replied, following him. "Makes me look more professional, or something. Right?" he pulled off his hat and ran his palm over the top of his bald head, and smoothed down the patches of close-shaved gray hair over his ears.

"Something like that," the guy said. He walked right over to the reporter, who had just finished with her makeup and was whipping her black hair behind her in preparation for the camera.

"Here's the guy," he said.

"Mr. Largess?" she asked. The cameraman and the sound guys were surrounding them.

"Yeah! Hi!" Matt said, beaming.

"Michelle Gonzalez."

"Yeah! I see you on the news all the time! Great!"

"Oh, thank you," said Michelle. "Thirty seconds? Okay. Thirty seconds," she said to Matt, seriously.

"What! You mean we're *on* in thirty seconds?"

"Don't worry, this is taped," she said.

Matt looked at her, confused.

"We're not live," she explained. "We tape this now and they'll play it later. If you really mess up an answer, or if *I* mess up we can start all over again. I usually go over it with you first but you're late, and we're pressed for time. It's Matthew, right? Arborist Matthew Largess?"

"Yeah," Matt said. "Oh... Mmmm-hmm! Matthew *Twig* Largess."

One of the sound guys called out. "And we're on in five, four..." He went silent and counted down to one on his fingers and then pointed his fingers at them.

Michelle put the microphone up to her mouth. "I'm joined now with Arborist Matthew... Largess, one of the advocates for the preservation of Oakland Forest. We're here at the entrance to the forest and you can see we are surrounded by homes. You may be able to see through the trees, off in the distance behind our cameras is a condominium complex. Mr. Largess, how is it possible that in the midst of all this development lies an area that had never been disturbed by man?"

"Well... I believe it was originally left undisturbed because it's wet," Matt said. "You can see the small stream right in front of us, and if you walk through there, you'll find a lot of areas of standing water. This type of land makes it harder to build on. Developers have to put more money into it to make it work. So they let it be and built where it was easier. Only now, there's nowhere else left to build. Look around," Matt said, gesturing with his palms up at all the houses around them. "There's nothing left.

If you took one of your helicopters up to look around, you'd see this is one of the only tracts of woods left on the Aquidneck Island. And it's the biggest. The biggest one left. You guys have a helicopter, right?"

"We do," said Michelle, and smiled strangely. "Mr. Largess," she continued, "Your opponents claim that the trees in this forest are not as old as you say they are. They say that this whole area was cleared when the surrounding neighborhood was built. How do you respond to that?"

"I say that I've cut through one of these trees myself, one that had fallen down, and counted over 200 rings in it. That means over 200 years old. That, right there, tells you that it *is* an old growth forest. And I'm getting scientists in here to take samples and get an exact age on the trees to verify this. *I'm* sure. *I* don't need the scientists; I've seen it with my own eyes. But people don't want to take my word for it. They want to hear it from the experts."

"Are you *not* an expert?"

"No, I am. I mean, *yes* I am. I'm a licensed arborist and I've studied trees my entire life. I graduated at the top of my class from Paul Smith Wilderness College. What I mean is, people want to hear it from the scientists. That makes the age of the trees a hard fact; to have scientific evidence."

"I see. And finally, why is it so important if these trees *are* indeed old?"

Matt looked at her like she was crazy.

"In other words," said Michelle, "Why is it more important to save a 200-year-old tree than, say, a sixty-year-old tree?"

"It means everything. The environment is the number one issue in the world today, and we're destroying it. We have holes in our ozone layer and greenhouse gasses all over the place. Trees are air purifiers. If we keep cutting it down… then there's going to be nothing left to filter out all the sh-- … pollution. And there's no place where it's more evident than this place, on this island, where this patch of woods is really the last thing left. And… to answer your question… a sixty-year-old tree is important to preserve as well, but it doesn't compare to something like this. These trees, the older trees provide habitat for wildlife that can't survive anywhere else except in an old growth forest. We have species dying because of this. Just look at the ivory-billed woodpecker. The Lord God Bird. Also, these trees grew this old because of the conditions that existed hundreds of years ago, before humans, or the white man, came here and messed everything up. Nowadays, we don't have those pristine conditions. So it's impossible for trees to grow like this, now. If we cut it, it's gone forever."

Michelle gave a big fake smile for the camera. "There you have it. I'm Michelle Gonzalez, Channel 10 News." She held the smile for an extra five seconds, staring at the camera.

"And…. We're out," called out one of the sound guys. "Okay, people! Let's pack it up and get a move on!"

Michelle handed the microphone over to one of her crew members and nodded at Matt. "Thank you, Mr. Largess," she said.

"Whoa. That's it?"

"That's it. You did great," she said.

"Did I really? I think if we did it again I could do a better job. I got sidetracked... started talking about helicopters, didn't I?"

"That's fine. We can cut that out. We'll probably only use a few lines of what you said, and you got plenty of good stuff in there. Thank you," she said, heading for the van. "And good luck."

Matt stood there, looking into the forest, while the crew packed everything into the van hurriedly. The whole thing was packed up within a couple minutes and the van started rolling out of the grass parking area.

"Hey!" Matt called out after them. "You forgot to call me 'Twig!' I want to have 'Twig' in there!"

The little reporter smiled awkwardly and waved to him, aware that he was calling after her but not willing to stop to hear him out.

"Mmmhmm," Matt whispered to himself. He shrugged his shoulders and began walking into the woods, eager to enjoy the last hour of daylight under the trees.

CHAPTER 12

The hawk was circling high above the forest in an open blue sky, gliding, with the tips of its wings looking like outstretched fingers scraping the sky.

"Red tail," Matt announced, craning his head back on his shoulders to look up through the beech branches. The branches were covered in green buds, ready to shoot forth the first leaves of spring at any moment. "Look at him. Looks likes he's circling *us*. Like he's stalking us like a mouse or something to scoop up. Rahr! Rahr!" He screeched, swiping his bent fingers through the air like talons.

The man walking next to him, Robert Muntz Ph.D. from the University of Rhode Island, looked over at him and chuckled. "That's quite good," he said. "You scared me. For a moment there I thought he was right on top of us."

Muntz was a gray-bearded man in his sixties with a gentle voice and a warming smile. He was an avid outdoorsman, donned in the newest, most expensive hiking garments on the market. He wore a light pack on his back, stuffed with the tools of his trade; the instruments for measuring, testing, and sampling trees.

Matt had on his chaps and a fleece jacket covered with sawdust and carried his medium-sized orange chain saw in his right hand, down by his thighs. He wore his muck-boots, unlaced and floppy even though they were hiking nearly a mile into the woods. His pale blue eyes lit up with electricity upon hearing Muntz' compliment.

"Mmmhmm! You like that? Yeah! Hey, Isn't this place awesome? I mean, don't you just feel like there's something special, here, just walking in here?"

"Well… it is peaceful," Muntz conceded.

"No, but I mean something more than that. Like… the first time I came in here I got the feeling like I was in church or something. And I still feel it a little bit every time I come in here. And I'm in here all the time, but it doesn't go away. Are you feeling any of that?"

"Well… no. Not yet, anyway. But this is my first time in here and you've been talking the whole time. So… maybe… if I was alone."

"Mmm… sorry. I do talk a lot. I got a mouth on me. People tell me that all the time. I'm a snake-oiler. A snake-oil salesman, like one of those old-fashioned guys who has to go door to door and get people to buy his stuff."

"Yes, I believe you have some of that in you. I saw your interview on the news. I thought you did a very good job."

Matt looked up to check on the hawk again and saw the bird land directly above them on the tip of one of the largest beeches in the forest.

"Look at that," Matt said. "He's probably waiting for us to scare some little critter out of the woodwork. That's what he's doing." Then, remembering what Muntz had said, he asked, "You really think I did okay on the news?"

"Excellent," said Muntz, looking Matt in the eye to let him know he meant it. "No one could have done it better. You explained the situation exactly how it is with little or no prejudice. And you spoke in a way that was scientific but at the same time familiar. In other words, like you're a regular guy who can explain things to other regular people. That's good. That's something *I* have to work on. My education gets the best of me sometimes; makes me sound pompous."

"I don't think so," Matt told him.

"Well… thank you. I *have* been working on it," the professor chuckled.

Up above them, the hawk let out a screech that pierced the sky and dove off the crown of the tree down into the lower branches of a tree nearer to them, following their progress. Then it sat perfectly still about thirty feet up, with the branches still shaking from the weight of its landing. It was a big one, about as big as a red tail can get, with a big broad chest atop a stocky body. It was well-fed and in the prime of its existence.

The two men stopped walking and looked up to study it.

"Magnificent," said Muntz. "I don't think I've ever seen one this close before."

"Me neither," said Matt. "He's cool. Look at him, up there. Seems like he likes us, doesn't he?"

"I'm not to sure about that," Muntz said, still studying the bird.

Matt squinted to get a better look and saw what Muntz was talking about. The bird had its dark black eyes pinned right on them and wasn't flinching.

"Mmm. Weird," Matt agreed.

The two of them stood there in silence, studying the hawk for a few moments before Matt spoke up.

"Mmmhmm!" he announced, and set back to hiking. "Yeah. Let's go. That tree is right around the bend in the trail here. See it? You can see forever in here; barely any brush. This is the one I was telling you about. The broken one that I counted the rings on."

"Right," Muntz said, following him.

They rounded the bend in the path and found the tree they were looking for. It was an old, thick beech that had broken at the base and was lying on the floor of the forest. There was a pile of sawdust around the its base, and the trunk had been cut flat by a chain saw. The circumference was large but not staggering; the two of them with their hands joined would be able to join fingers easily.

"Here we go," Matt said. "I didn't cut it down. It was broken. See?" he asked, pointing to the portion of the trunk with a jagged, torn end that lay on the ground a few feet off.

"I never doubted you," Muntz said.

Muntz knelt down on the ground, flipped the pack off his back and began going through it. He pulled out a few small bottles full of liquids of different colors, some clear and some more bronze in hue. He had thick plastic collecting bags and some metal instruments, one of which looked like a protractor. He laid all of these things out on top of the compacted mat of leaves a few feet away from the base of the tree.

"You can go ahead and cut me off a slice. I'll need a fresh cut, anyway," he said.

Matt took the orange guard off the bar and pulled out the choke on the saw. "How big?" he asked.

"About two inches thick would be perfect. I need it sturdy enough so it won't break apart while we're testing it but not so heavy that we have to break our backs to get it out of here."

"You got it," Matt said.

He grabbed the starter cord and bent his knees to give it a rip, but before he could do so he was startled upright by another shriek from the hawk. Only this time, it was closer and clearer than before and almost deafening in its intensity. And when Matt turned around to look for it, he found out just how close it was. It was no more than ten feet away from him, swooping down with its wings out wide and its talons poised under its body.

Matt didn't even have time to curse. He dropped his saw, put his hands up over his head and ducked just in time for the bird to sail over the top of him. It was close enough that he could feel the wind rush by his head. He looked up after it to see it arc back upwards towards the sky, check its speed with a graceful twist of its wings, and set down on a lower branch of beech tree close to them. Then the bird sat there, glaring at Matt with its black eyes and its hooked beak.

Matt looked down at the professor, who was kneeling down by his pack and looking up at him.

"Did you see that?" Matt whispered.

Muntz nodded.

"Do you think he's going to do that again?"

Muntz shrugged his shoulders. "It's odd behavior. Maybe it's got a nest close to here, and is protecting its territory."

"Maybe," Matt said. He looked down at his saw, picked it up and examined it. "Maybe he doesn't want me to cut the tree."

"What do you mean?" asked Muntz, confused.

"I don't know… just seems like that," Matt snapped. He was angry with himself for saying it, and confused by feeling it. "What? You want a piece? Fine! I'll cut you a piece!"

Matt yanked on the starter and the saw coughed to life with the first pull. He revved the motor up only briefly as he squatted down over the stump, and then pushed the chain into the tree. The chain was sharp and was making fast work of it. Matt focused on his work until he got about halfway through, when he allowed himself to steal a peek at the hawk. It was still right where he left it, staring down at him from thirty feet away. He shook his head and focused back on his work, and kept at it until the chain came through the other side of the trunk and the two-inch-thick specimen spun free on top of the bar.

Matt kicked the chunk off the top of the stump and looked back up at the hawk. It was still there, taunting him.

He took off, running at it with the saw down by his side. "Go on! Get outa here!" he bellowed, stomping on the ground and waving his arm frantically to scare the bird off.

The hawk sat completely still and patiently waited for Matt to finish his tirade. When he was done, the hawk stared at him for another five seconds before something clicked in its brain. Its head moved side to side with the usual quick-ticking neck movements of a bird, and the bird lifted off the branch. With a few powerful strokes of its wings it was propelled up above the tree line and flew off into the brightness of the sun.

Matt watched it go until he was blinded by the sun and couldn't see it anymore. He put his hand up to rub the vision back into his eyes.

"That was strange," Muntz said. "I've never seen a bird act like that before. It was as if it were in a trance or something. Very peculiar."

"Yeah," Matt said, rubbing his eyes and blinking. "Mmmhmm! See? That's what I'm talking about! This place is special! There's something about this place! See? I told you!"

Muntz chuckled again and went back to work with his instruments. "I see," he said.

"Do you?" Matt asked, incredulously. He stormed over to the stump and kicked the newly cut slab of wood with his toe. "Look at this! Look at the fucking rings in this thing! Count 'em! Go ahead! Count 'em!"

Muntz squinted at him. It was the first trace of concern Matt had seen on his face all day. "I will," he said calmly. "When I get back to the lab."

"Okay," Matt said, calming. "I'm just saying… I mean… tell me what you think. Just *looking* at this place and *looking* at this stump. You *know* that this is a virgin forest, don't you? I mean… you've seen them before. You're an expert. Don't you just know it?"

"It certainly displays some of the characteristics of an old growth forest, yes. And I can see there are a great deal of rings in this stump. But there are other factors to consider… things that can be deceiving. That's why we do the tests. I'm a scientist, Matt. I don't just *look---*"

Muntz broke off and squinted again, this time looking somewhere over Matt's shoulder. "Are you expecting someone?" he asked.

Matt turned around to see a man off in the near distance, walking towards them on the trail at a stiff pace. As the man got closer and came into focus, Matt recognized him. It was Jim Trent, the guy from the development group with whom he'd initially discussed the project.

"Hey! Jim!" Matt called out jovially. "Yeah! What's happenin'?"

"You're trespassing," Trent called back to him, walking hard at him.

"Huh?" Matt responded.

"You're trespassing," Trent repeated, walking up and off the trail to stand before Matt. He was wearing an overcoat, pressed slacks, and brand new white sneakers that were covered in muck from the walk.

"Aw, man. You got your new shoes all muddy," Matt said, genuinely.

Trent shook his head and sighed. He produced a white envelope from the pocket of his overcoat and extended it out towards Matt.

"For me?" Matt asked.

Trent nodded. "Consider yourself *served,*" he said.

Matt watched the corner of his mouth twitch after he spoke and his beady dark eyes widen behind his thick-rimmed glasses. Matt got the sense that he was enjoying himself; that he'd been waiting for this.

"You and your friend here are trespassing on private property," he continued. I'll be notifying the police when I get back to my car. I suggest you be gone before they get here."

"Aw, man. Why do you have to be like that?" Matt asked.

"Take the papers," Trent said.

Matt looked at the envelope, hanging there in front of him in Trent's hand. Reluctantly, he grabbed it out from between his fingers.

"Good afternoon, Mr. Largess," Trent said, and without hesitation turned on his heels and began walking away.

Matt watched him go for a moment before he ripped into the envelope to see what was inside.

"Friend of yours?" asked the professor, who was busy working on the tree trunk with his instruments.

"I guess not," said Matt, looking at the first page of the letter. "You know what this is? It's a court order." He read aloud exactly the way his mind interpreted any documents laden with legal terms: "Matthew Largess... blah blah blah... cease and desist from making unprecedented and slanderous comments about blah blah blah... some lot number or something... being an old growth or virgin forest on to any media source... blah blah blah... in particular Channel 10 News, The Newport Times and The Providence Journal."

Matt looked up from the papers. "Wow! I've never gotten something like this before. Is it bad? Can they do that?"

"Evidently so," said Muntz, who appeared to be working quickly with his instruments and tubes of chemicals. "I'm here, and I'm not leaving without these samples. I'll be five minutes... at the most."

Matt smiled at him. "Take your time," he said, taking a seat right down on the forest floor. He rested back on his elbows and crossed his legs at the ankles. "I've been arrested for worse."

CHAPTER 13

I don't remember the exact details of this night, as I was whacking down tumblers of Maker's Mark one after the other like they were jelly beans, but what I do remember is as follows:

I was sitting at the bar of a little Italian restaurant, drinking with my most formidable all-time drinking partner, Jack R. Deldon. Deldon was good for a lot of reasons, but the two best were that he always wanted to drink when I did and he usually got sloppier than me, making me look like a true champion. He was a single sportsman, a slayer of females. The theme of our drinking bout that evening, the one we kept inevitably coming back to, was that I was going to make a terrific father. He said he was jealous of me; that he would trade in all his conquests and debauchery to have a woman like my Courtney and have a little baby on the way.

The bar was the Ristorante in town. They had an outside bar that was all under a big, high awning. There were space heaters set up around the bar and white Christmas lights strung all over the place. It was a nice place for a cocktail, especially on a mild Spring evening like this one where the air was just cool enough for the space heaters to cozy you up.

I remember feeling really good about it for the first time. I mean, I went through my spells of getting excited but then I'd always slip back into being nervous about it. I don't know what the hell I was nervous about. I just was. I guess it's because I fear change, in general. I'm a simple man. So, this was the first time I felt truly at peace with being a dad. I remember sitting there, laughing and smiling and feeling just great about the hand life had dealt me, with the whiskey making a warm, snuggly spot in the pit of my belly.

That's why it was so strange that the night ended the way it did.

In between one of our repetitive segments of discussing how great of a dad I was going to be, we somehow got on the subject of Matt. I suppose I was telling a story about him, and we were laughing. We must have been pretty loud, as a patron from a few seats away decided to jump in on our conversation.

"That guy's a fucking retard," he said.

It was Chris Head, a local carpenter and drunkard. The Ristorante was an L-shaped bar, and he was sitting a few seats from the corner on the other side, so I could see him perfectly. It's funny that his last name is Head because he has a giant head and he wears his hair in a ponytail. You can see his head bouncing up the street from a mile away. He was a jovial guy who I'd never seen upset or serious about anything. That is, until now.

I don't know if it was the whiskey or what, but it seemed to me like he had a real problem with what I was saying, like he had some deep-seeded grudge against Matt.

"*You're* a fucking retard!" I hollered, and stood up out of my bar seat. (Looking back on it, I see just how sophisticated of an argument it was, indeed.)

It escalated quickly. He looked like he wanted to go so I rushed right at him and form-tackled him just as he managed to get out of his seat. I crashed down on top of him with all my weight and drove him down into the gravel floor.

The rest was kind of like a scrum in a rugby match, from my recollection. We were both rolling around on the ground trying to get an arm free enough to get a good shot in, but neither of us really did. There were probably five or six people trying to pull us apart, so every time one of us did break free for a second we were restrained.

After a minute or two one of us, or both of us (I don't recall) bumped into one of the tall propane-fueled space heaters and knocked it to the ground. I remember looking up from underneath Chris and seeing the gravel on fire around the thing from the gas it had spilled out. The next thing I knew, we weren't fighting anymore and someone was spraying a fire extinguisher on the flames.

After that, everyone cleared out into the street while they waited for the fumes to get carried out from underneath the awning. Deldon suggested we should get out of there, and I agreed without an argument. It was nice to have *him* looking out for *me* for a change. We walked back to my apartment, cracked a couple cold ones, and sat at the patio table in my backyard. I lived right in town.

From there, we could see through the trees down to the main drag where the bars were so we watched and waited to see if the cops came. I figured if they did, I'd walk back down there and deal with whatever I had coming to me. Whatever they did to me it would be better than waking my wife up on a work night and having to deal with her wrath.

Thankfully, the cops never came. Regretfully, Deldon and I were so loud that we woke my wife up anyway. And yes, I felt her wrath.

When I woke up the next day in the middle of the afternoon feeling like there were needles behind my eyeballs and my tongue was coated in ashes, one of the first things I wondered about was why that particular comment from The Head had sent me over the edge. It's not like he was talking junk about my wife, my mom, or even me. It was just Matt. *Mickey*. The guy who pissed me off to the point where I had to walk off his job. So, why?

A wise man once told me that the truth comes out when you're drunk. Life experiences have shown me that when it comes to other people, this isn't quite true. I've met people who are pretty nice people who sometimes get all nasty when they're drunk. In these cases, it isn't anything close to the truth that comes out. It's more like some kind of hideous monster that's nothing like the person's true self. But in my case, for the most part, it's true.

I guess I felt bad about the way things went down. I regretted it, even.

Well, springtime broke through and I was off and running with my landscaping business, chasing the American dream. I was building something out of nothing, running around town passing out business cards and running ads in the local paper (the same one I used to write for). Soon enough, I had a little bit of work to show for all my efforts. It wasn't enough to keep me busy every day of the week, but it was enough to keep some money in my pocket until I got it going nice.

It was one of the first early Spring days that I had something to work on when I first saw Matt since I told him where he could stick it. I was working right on the side of the road on North Road, transplanting some daylillies in front of a stone wall to soften up the wall and make the entry to the driveway a little more inviting. I was going at it pretty hard, picking away with my shovel in a full sweat, when I heard the truck tires turning through the sand on the side of the road. It was Matt in his little black truck, pulling off the road to talk to me.

He rolled down the passenger side window and leaned way over in the seat.

"Hey! Shame! What's happening? Yeah!" he called out.

He was wearing a floppy safari-type hat with a long brim on it, so he had to lean down low in the seat to make eye contact with me between the small gap in the brim and the window of the truck. He was sporting a big, goofy grin.

"What's up, dude?" I asked, leaning on my shovel. I decided to get right into it. "Hey, I been meaning to tell you... sorry about blowing up on you and everything. I—"

He was waving me off before I even started, and kept shooing at me while I was talking. "Forget it," he said, cutting me off. "It's nothing. So how are you? You busy? You got work?"

"I got work, some days. But I'm not busy."

"I'll tell you what," he said, scratching his chin. "I need a couple retaining walls built at my house. That'd probably be perfect for you. You can work there whenever you want, like whenever you got nothing else going on. It's probably weeks worth of work. It'll keep you busy. So what do you say? Huh? Yeah?"

I shrugged my shoulders. "Sure. Sounds great."

"Yeah. You know how to do that stuff... building stone walls?"

"Sure," I said. "Nothing to it." This was only a little white lie. I had worked on walls before but never single-handedly constructed one from start to finish. It was going to take a little bit of research.

At this point, a shiny new silver BMW sedan came speeding over the crest of the hill and then slowed down slightly as it prepared to pass us. "Treehugger!" screamed the driver through the crack in his tinted window, the last syllables trailing off as the car sped past us.

I looked at Matt, who was squinting off after the car. "You gonna take that?" I asked.

"Yeah. Tony Marchietti. Doctor. He's pissed because I'm trying to save an American Elm he wants to cut down in his front yard for no fucking reason. He says it's dropping sticks on his precious beamer. I say it's on town property, 'cause it's next to the road, and I told the town about it. We'll see what happens."

"Right," I said.

"Yeah. Good. Mmmhmm!" he declared, changing gears. "That'll help get you going. It works out good 'cause I need it done anyway and I want to help you get going."

"Cool."

"Yeah. So how's the book coming?"

"Oh," I said, and hesitated because I didn't remember telling him anything about the book I was writing. It was a Don Quixote-type thing about a senile old man called *The Memoirs of Sergeant Steamer.* "Pretty good," I ventured.

"Yeah! You started it and everything?" he asked, with his eyes popping to life and twinkling under his floppy brim.

"Wait... what book are you talking about?"

"Come on! The one about *me*! About saving the forest!"

I couldn't find anything to say, so I just stared at him.

"You told me and Eleanor you were going to write it! Don't you remember?"

"Yeah... but—"

"But nothing. That's bullshit! You said you were writing it! I can't believe you haven't even started! Are you serious?"

I laughed. *Here we go, again,* I thought. "I just said I was writing it so there'd be a reason for me to be with you that day. I don't know why..."

Matt was disgusted. He sighed and looked straight ahead out his front windshield before looking back at me.

"Okay I gotta go," blurted out quickly. "Come by my house and I'll show you the work. I gotta go. Mmmhmm!"

And with that he looked over his shoulder to check for traffic and was off, back out onto North Road. He drove aggressively, winding through the gears and was quickly out of sight over the crest of the hill.

There was no more traffic on the road. Everything was calm and peaceful, like it was before. I stood there for a minute, leaning on my shovel, trying to digest some of that whirlwind, then plunged it back into the rocky soil.

CHAPTER 14

Matt sat at his desk in the basement, amidst the clutter of one thousand sheets of loose perforated computer paper penned with random notes and telephone numbers, and stared at the big yellow envelope in his hands. He was both afraid to open it and curious to see what was inside. He could feel the energy running through the thing. It was practically jumping out of his hands. There was something weird about it, that was for sure. The return address explained all of this in the two words on the top line: *Crystal Powers.*

Maybe it'd be better to just chuck it in the trash right now, before he even opened it. He could pretend he thought it was junk mail and be done with it; act like it never happened. All this stuff about angels and all the prophecies--- it was all too weird. He had enough to think about without the supernatural creeping in on the mix. He should be focusing on the science and the legal issues of the thing; about proving that the forest was as old as he knew it was and about finding the right documents and procedures to save it. Anything else was a waste of time. All this nonsense, all it could do was take time away from the things he should be focusing on.

Matt pushed away from his desk and slid across the room on his wheeled office chair and steadied the envelope over the trash basket. He held it there, thinking hard about it, but curiosity got the best of him. He had to at least take a peek at what was inside. He had to find out if all that perceived energy that was making the envelope tremble in his hands was from all the hype about his meeting with Crystal or from something that was actually inside. He tore it open quickly and slid out the contents.

There were two sheets of paper inside. The first was a note handwritten on a piece of yellow-lined legal paper. It was all done in beautiful, legible cursive handwriting. It read:

Dear Matthew,

My visions have shown me that you have received the ancient hawk warning. The hawk you saw in the forest was trying to warn you that danger was approaching you that day. Only someone who's very close to nature can receive such a warning. The Native Americans who once ruled over this land understood this very well. I tell you this only so you can understand how close you are getting. The forest accepts you as a part of itself whenever you enter.

Here is the first of the blessings I'll be sending you. It can be delivered by YOU, and you only. You'll need to take it into the heart of the forest and tuck it somewhere under the leaf-litter on the forest floor. This is the only way it will be received.

I know that you have your doubts about this but please follow my instructions, for the sake of the forest. This is a very powerful blessing that will provide much needed protection. I know you will do the right thing. Thank you and good luck,

Crystal Powers

p.s. Remember you are the voice of the forest! It can't speak for itself!

p.s.s. Angels will rise out of the forest floor to rejoice once the forest is saved!

Matt shrugged his shoulders and peeled away the sheet of note paper to reveal the blessing. It was a thick, brownish hued paper with soft edges that looked like it was from the middle ages. It was decorated by beautiful, color drawings of life-like quality. There was a picture of a small branch of a beech tree, with copper-colored leaves hanging onto the twigs. There was a picture of an angel with soft, white wings crowned with a golden halo. The angel had golden hair, rosy cheeks, and sorrowful eyes lifted towards the heavens. There was a small image of a bluish-colored flower; something he recalled seeing sprouting up from amidst a cluster of ground-cover in the forest. And there was a picture of a female deer walking under the trees with two baby deer.

At the center of all this were the following words, penned in exquisite calligraphy.

Blessed are the trees
Blessed are the spirits within
Blessed is the earth
The womb where sweet, full life begins

Upon glancing briefly at the blessing and reading these words, Matt was moved. His breath was taken away from him for a moment, and as soon as it came back he set into motion. All at once, his feeling about it changed completely. There was only one thing to do. He had to go to the forest as soon as possible and follow Crystal's instructions.

Matt was out of the house in ten seconds and into his little black pickup, speeding towards the forest.

❧

A few days later, Matt and I went walking through the forest in search of the spot where he said he left the blessing. It was a clear, cloudless day in the full-on heat of July, right about the beginning of the real nasty heat, the kind that had you sweating from the time you rolled out of bed in the morning. The summer weeds were reaching head-high in the open field that buffered the forest from the surrounding neighborhood. Bits of pokeweed and briars leapt out of the meadow and into the path where we walked. Matt barreled through them with his kevlar chaps, and I kept close to his back so I wouldn't get nailed with the whiplash.

"You're paying me for this, right?" I asked him.

"C'mon. Hurry up! Mmmhmm!" he said, and kept trucking. He was leaning into it, like he was being sucked by a magnet towards the opening in the forest.

"Maybe you didn't hear me. I said—"

"Yeah, I heard you. Yeah, fine. Jesus, is that all you care about? We're talking about magic, here. We're talking about whether there's still magic in this world. Don't you think that's interesting?"

"Yeah. It's just..." I hesitated here, feeling a little guilty.

"Just what?" he snapped.

"I think it's cool. But I can't be dicking around today. I have a hedge to cut where I could be making 300 bucks right now, that's all I'm saying. I have to work."

"Relax," he said. "I'm paying you. It's research. You're working."

"Fair enough," I said.

We trudged our way through the path on the outskirts of the big meadow until we came to a small stream, no more than four feet wide, that ran the length of the meadow, separating the forest from the meadow. After a short time walking along the bank of the stream we came upon a couple of planks laid over the water and crossed over them to the other side.

"You feel that?" Matt asked.

I was about to ask him what he was talking about when I felt it. It was like the temperature dropped ten degrees the moment I stepped off the planks onto the other bank. The air had a coolness to it in the shade and the ground felt moist under my feet. There were no head-high weeds on this side. There were only tree roots, barren ground, and leaf-litter. There were some patches of low-bush blueberry and ground cover close to the bank, but as we walked in deeper there was basically nothing but the trees.

I looked up and around at the trees and was surprised to find that they really weren't that big. I'd say the biggest ones I could see were maybe fifty or sixty feet tall. I was expecting to see hundred-foot beeches with trunks ten feet in diameter, because that's how the really old ones in front of the mansions in Newport were. None of these were like that. I figured that I must not be seeing the whole picture; maybe this was just the outer rim and the big fatties were in the middle or something. So I strained my eyes to look through the forest as far as I could. All I saw stretching forever was tree trunks. There were no low branches on the trees at all and very little brush, so I could see forever in there. What I saw next was just as strange to me. Far across the forest, through the midst of all the trunks, there was a freshly painted white house with blue shutters and a swing-set in the back yard. I could barely make it out off in the distance but it was there. And then others came into view around it. This place wasn't that big at all. It was only a few acres, twenty at most, sitting right in the middle of two neighborhoods.

I chuckled to myself and looked up for Matt, who was a good fifty yards in front of me by then, full steam ahead. I didn't know whether to laugh or cry. To me, it was obvious that this forest wasn't as old as he was saying it was. Just looking at it, the trees weren't that big and there were houses all over the place. You'd have to be nuts to see it any other way.

And that's when it hit me. Matt Largess was insane. I'd always known he was a little weird and crazy, but I thought he had at least some portion of his mind grounded in reality. After all, he ran a successful business, he was a good father to his kids, he showered and put on clean clothes like everyone else (except for the chaps, but that was more of an outer layer… I'm assuming… I hope). But *this*. *This* was proof to the contrary. It was like he'd conjured up this dream about the trees here being older than anywhere else and full of magic and he wanted it to be true so badly that he had himself convinced. It was an obsession.

I didn't know what to do. I had all but stopped walking as the realization came to me, and now I stopped and stood there. I heard the slight breeze rustling through the beech leaves and the stream trickling in the background. And I could barely hear Matt clomping his boots on the ground up ahead on the path.

Part of me was freaked out. I thought about turning around and walking back to my truck by myself. I was out in the woods with this guy with no one else around. What if today was the day he finally went off the deep end? He probably had some kind of saw or pruner strapped to him somewhere. He could slice me up and leave me for dead. He could probably bludgeon me to death with a downed limb, or his bare brutish hands for that matter. Then I'd never be a daddy… I'd never be anything. Just a pile of blood and guts.

But he wasn't going to do that. He was harmless. It was just all so sad and strange to me. One thing was for sure; I wasn't going to ruffle his feathers out here. Maybe I could confront him about it later, back in society where there were witnesses around. But not now. For now I had to be cool and play along with him.

"Let's GO!" Matt called back to me, his voice echoing through the forest. "C'mon! What the hell are you doing back there?"

"All right," I called back weakly, not knowing whether it was loud enough for him to hear me but unwilling to repeat myself. I picked up the pace and walked briskly along the path, on the cool ground of the forest. It was silent and peaceful in there, without any sounds of traffic or machinery of the modern world. My footsteps seemed strangely loud to me, and the rustle of the leaves in between my steps formed a meditative rhythm.

I suddenly felt pretty good. Despite everything, I was glad I came out. It was good for me. I'd spent a good deal of time hiking and mountain biking when I was in college but I hadn't been out in the woods in a long time. Now I remembered why I used to like it so much. I kind of lost track of time for a minute there, listening to the swoosh-plop of my feet on the path and thinking about old times.

After a while I heard something interrupt my rhythm, like an animal rooting around in the leaves and making some weird grunting noises. I looked up to find Matt on his hands and knees, scraping layers of leaves away from the forest floor. He reminded me of a big overgrown skunk digging for grubs. I could hear him going, "Mmmhmm! Mmmhmm!" in a low grumble under his breath.

Be cool, I reminded myself. *Don't piss him off.* I walked over to him but kept my distance, about ten feet away.

"It's gone!" He proclaimed, looking up at me from down on all fours, with his face bright red and his eyes about to shine right out of his head. The leaves were all torn up in a radius twenty feet around him, with the damp black undersides mounded in clumps on the surface. His bare hands were covered in muck. "Poof! Gone!" he exclaimed, looking up at me and awaiting a response.

I shrugged my shoulders.

Matt pushed himself up to his feet and wiped his hands on his thighs. "Tell me you don't believe in magic now, you fucker!"

I laughed and shuffled my feet. "Are you sure you're looking in the right spot? It's pretty big out here."

"Of course I am," he snapped. "Look. There's the mother beech," He said, pointing to a large tree off to his left. "You see how there's no other trees growing around it? How it's all clear in here with no chutes or anything all around it?"

I looked around and saw what he was saying. There was a clear area in the forest all around it, and looking up I noticed that the branches started lower to the ground than any of the others. "Yeah," I said.

"Well I put the thing right *here*," he said, gesturing down by his feet, "two days ago. And now it's gone."

He looked at me again, this time with an *I told you so* face.

"You put a piece of paper in the woods two days ago, and now it's gone," I said.

"Is that nuts, or what? Tell me that's not magic. Go ahead. Tell me."

I took a deep breath while I tried to figure how to handle this one. "It could be. I'll give you that."

"Thank you. This is amazing! This forest is saved! I can feel it! Can't you feel it? Oh my God! It's kind of freaky, isn't it? Are you freaked out, a little bit?"

"I don't know," I said. "Now, don't get all pissed off. But I'm just saying… and just think about this for a minute… it was a piece of paper. What if the wind blew it away?"

He shook his head. "No. I tucked it way under the leaves. *Way* under. Like three inches. You see how thick this shit is? No way."

"All right," I conceded, though I still didn't believe him. "What if you're not looking in the right spot?"

"I *am* looking in the right spot. I put it on the north side of the tree, twenty paces away. This is north," he said, holding his arm out. "Wait. Or is it this way?" he asked, pointing in a slightly different direction. "*Here!*" he shouted. "Look *here!*" He fell to his knees and started rummaging around right next to all the ripped up leaves. "C'mon! Don't just stand there! Help!"

I didn't like when he started barking at me like this. So I walked over there and started kicking all the leaves up with my boots. I was searching with a purpose, too, not just going through the motions. I wanted to find this thing and wave it right in front of his face and ask him how he liked his magic, now.

Matt pushed himself up, out of breath, and wiped his hands clean again. "You're fucking with me," he said. "Stop it. I was looking in the right place the first time. I know it."

"Fine," I said, frustrated. "Then let's go. Freekin' unsolved mysteries. Call up the TV crew."

"You don't believe me, do you?" he asked, and stood there looking at me with his crazy sparkling eyes.

I felt bad for him, again. "Look," I said. "I want to believe you. To think that something magic is happening…

that's really cool. I'm into it. But you have to think about what else could have happened, too. The wind could have gotten it. You could be looking in the wrong spot."

"No," he said. "That's not what happened."

"All right."

"Mmmhmm. That's okay. I don't care if you believe it. It happened. Mmmhmm! Okay. I saw what I had to see. Let's go. C'mon! Let's GO!" he barked. He had already started walking out.

I laughed because I didn't know what else to do. "I thought you weren't mad at me," I said.

"I'm not mad at you. You're my writer. Are you hungry? I'm hungry. I'll take you out for lunch instead of paying you. How's that?"

I sighed. "Sounds great," I said, and followed him down the trail.

CHAPTER 15

The Portsmouth Town Hall was a hundred year-old building that had undergone plenty of refurbishment over the years but still retained its primitive character. Many of the old 6x6 posts and beams were still exposed and its floors were comprised of knotty, uneven pine planks. The meeting hall was a great open room lined with bookcases stocked full of bound volumes of zoning decisions, maps and bylaws. The room carried a person's voice, or any noise, well and added a touch of extra bass behind a slight echo, making even an old granny sound like Abraham Lincoln.

There were three long tables lined up at one end of the meeting hall, behind which sat the Town Administrator and various other people of importance. On a usual evening there were thirty or forty chairs clustered a few feet away from the panel, half of which were empty, leaving the greater portion of the large hall vacant. Tonight, the chairs were full and the people were packed into the great room shoulder to shoulder, filling it to capacity.

Seated in the front row on one side were Jim Trent and his business associates, all dressed in suits and ties and looking very serious. Trent's attorney, Seth Weinstein, sat directly next to him. He was a round man with slicked back black hair, wearing an exquisite charcoal gray Armani suit coupled with a loud, hot red tie. On the other side of the isle sat Matt in his finest overall chaps and a T-shirt, smiling confidently. He had reason to be excited, as Professor Muntz was explaining his scientific findings to the panel. Eleanor was seated next to Matt with a concerned look on her soft, angelic face. She had her hands clasped together in the lap of her long black skirt, and was wringing them together nervously.

"So, to explain the documents you're all looking at in layman's terms," Muntz was saying, "basically, our tests have concluded that the tree we tested is, or was, exactly 238 years old. This does, by definition, classify it as old growth."

Matt pumped his fist down by his waist in his seat.

"Further," Muntz continued, as he pushed his glasses up the bridge of his nose, "it is more than reasonable to conclude that the entirety of Oakland Forest is an old growth forest. The chances that we have selected the single oldest tree in the forest are slim... in other words it is my opinion that the oldest tree in this forest may be close to 300 years old. Also, the chances that there could be one old tree and no others is, in this case, impossible. It is a fact, proven by these findings and backed by myself and the University of Rhode Island, that this area in question is indeed classified as an old growth forest."

"Yeah, baby! Yeah!" Matt roared, unable to contain himself any longer. He rocked back and forth in his seat excitedly and panned the faces of all the town representatives seated in the panel, as a few chuckles and hoots escaped from the crowd of bystanders.

Town Administrator Robert Ginnerty, who was presiding over the meeting, shot Matt a look of reproach before he spoke. He was a ruddy, slender sixty-year-old man with a thick crop of white hair and a slender face. "Thank you, professor," he said. "In light of this evidence, the board moves to resolve this point of controversy regarding this case, and accept that the area in question *is* an old growth forest. Mr. Weinstein, do you have any objection to this?"

Weinstein leaned over close to Jim Trent's seat as Trent whispered something in his ear.

"We do not," Weinstein announced.

"Then the board hereby concludes that Oakland Forest *is* an old growth forest." Ginnerty banged his gavel down on the striking block, tossed it on the table carelessly, and began shuffling through the packet of papers before him. "Now, moving on to agenda item 4a entitled 'Recommendations of the Town Planning Department...'"

Matt's smile faded into a placid look of bewilderment, and then turned downward into a scowl. His big frame trembled with rage, causing the legs of his aluminum folding chair to clatter against the old plank wood floor.

"We'd like to first consider the document with the approval from the Town Planner, dated January 16, in which—"

"*Approval!*" Matt roared, springing up out of his seat. His face was bright red and white foam bubbled at the corner of his mouth. "*Documents!* What the hell are you talking about? *Case closed! Case closed!*"

The room grew more silent than it had been all night. Eleanor reached up to grab Matt's hand in an effort to settle him down, but Matt snapped his hand away and stared Ginnerty down.

"Excuse me?" said Ginnerty, startled by the unexpected outburst.

"Didn't you just hear what the professor said? Didn't you hear what *you* said? *It's old growth! Case closed! That's it!*"

Now the crowd came to life, with the majority present declaring their approval of Matt's sentiment. Ginnerty buried his forehead in his hand and leaned his elbow forward on the table in front of him. Then he struck his gavel three times, loudly. "Mr. Largess, sit down," he ordered.

Matt stood there and considered it for a moment, until he realized that every eye in the place was on him and nothing was going to happen until he took his seat. He stepped back and plopped himself hard into his seat, and then slid forward so his ass was barely touching the front of it. He was nearly squatting over the seat; there may have been a sliver of air between them.

Eleanor put her hand on Matt's knee. "Matt. Calm down," she whispered.

"First of all, you are out of order. Secondly, you---"

Matt burst right out of his seat for the second time. "How can you just sit there and pretend like nothing even happened? The findings of the Planning Board are all old!

All of it… It's all old now! This case should be closed, *right now!*"

Now the crowd was incensed. The murmuring escalated into a near raucous. Ginnerty banged his gavel repeatedly, and all of the commotion only fueled Matt's fire. He bellowed louder than anyone else in the building.

"You're gonna let this happen, now, knowing what you know? It's a crime against humanity! It's a fucking crime, is what it is!"

Now it was Ginnerty's turn to get red in the face. He pounded his gavel as hard as he could, missing the striking plate and rattling papers loose all over the table. The dramatic effect silenced the crowd.

"Mr. Largess!" Ginnerty shouted, with more vigor than he'd displayed in over twelve years of service as Town Administrator. "You are hereby ordered to leave this meeting immediately! And let that be a lesson to all of you," he said, leveling his gavel accusingly at the crowd. "This type of outburst will not be tolerated. *That,* Mr. Largess, *is* a crime, for which you can be jailed. If you don't want to leave this place of your own will *right now,* there is a police officer at the door who would be glad to assist you."

Matt took a breath and prepared to lash back at him.

"Not another word. I'm warning you," Ginnerty threatened.

Matt felt the eyes on him. The entire panel was looking at him, hoping he'd say something else.

Eleanor stood up, flattened the front of her floor-length skirt, and stepped up close to Matt's side. She was so calm, she seemed on the verge of smiling, just as she always was. There was softness in her eyes.

"Come on," she said. "I'll walk out with you."

Matt looked at her and smiled, then turned back to the panel and let every one of them see the grin on his face. Then, smartly, he exited the building with Eleanor by his side without saying another word. It was a longer walk out than it had been on the way in, that's for sure. He didn't bother looking at anyone who stared him down as he left; he just kept his eyes focused on the big oak doors and held his head high.

Outside, the night air was warm and heavy. When the humidity set in on the summer heat in Rhode Island it was suffocating. They stood on the landing of the big stone steps that led up to the old oak doors of the Town Hall, flanked by the ancient yew bushes that protected the façade of the building. Matt felt the heaviness of the air as he tried to breathe to calm himself down. The air, coupled with his anxiety, wouldn't let him get a clean breath.

"I just don't understand how the fuck they can do this," Matt said, staring out into the parking lot.

"Matthew," Eleanor said softly.

Matt was slightly startled by the sound of her voice. He had forgotten she was with him. He had forgotten everything, except the echoing of the words spoken in the last five minutes.

"This may not be the best time to scold you...," she said, "but you really should learn to watch your language a bit."

Matt had never seen this look from her before. She didn't exactly look like she was mad, but she looked like she meant what he was saying.

"Why? Did I swear?" asked Matt.

Eleanor nodded. "You did. You just did here in front of me and you screamed it in front of everyone inside."

"I did?"

"Yes. You have a mouth like a sailor, Matthew. It's like a crutch for you... the way you use the F-word. Certain people, as in most of the people who you need to listen to you on this one, are going to tune you out as soon as they hear it."

"Mmmhmm," Matt said. He shuffled his boots around on the stone landing. "I *am* a sailor. What can I do about that?"

Eleanor pretended not to hear him. "Other than that... you didn't do so poorly. I wouldn't be ashamed of yourself, getting booted out like this."

"No?"

"No. At least the people see how passionate you are. That's good. It makes them want to be passionate about it, too. Did you hear the way they reacted, once you got going?"

Matt grinned. "Sounded like they were on our side, most of 'em."

Eleanor showed him her soft smile for a moment before cautioning him again. "You really must watch your language, though. *That's* the only thing *I* would be embarrassed about." With that, she started with her petite, measured footsteps down the stone staircase. "Goodnight, Matthew," she said.

"Wait!" Matt called out.

She held onto the iron railing and turned back to him.

"I just.... I don't understand how you can be so calm about this. I don't understand any of it. I mean... we just proved our point. That should be it. How can they even still be talking in there? There's no *way* they can build on that land now."

Eleanor looked up at him compassionately. "Did you really think it would end, just like that?"

Matt shrugged. "Well... it *should*."

Eleanor giggled. "I'm sorry," she said. "I'm not laughing at you. That's how simple it should be, you're right. But this is only one small step for us. It's important and necessary, yes... but just because we've identified what we're dealing with doesn't mean that the forest is saved. There are no laws that protect old growth from being developed. At least, none that are strong enough."

"So... what does that mean? What's the use, then? I mean... are we doing all this for no fucking reason?"

Eleanor shook her head. "You did it again," she said.

Matt wondered what she was talking about, then realized. He wasn't in the mood for this, right now. He waved her off. "I know, I know. I'll work on it, all right? So, what does it mean? Help me out, here. I'm pissed off."

"It's all going to come down to money. You knew that all along, didn't you? Isn't that why you contacted *me* in the first place?"

Matt looked her in confusion. "No," he said.

Eleanor saw that he meant what he was saying, and marveled at it.

"I came to you because you've saved forests before. Because you know what you're doing."

"I saved those forests with my money, and by getting other wealthy people and agencies to contribute as well."

"Oh," said Matt, looking more hurt than confused.

"You realize that money's not the only part of it. What you're doing is equally important. It can't work without what you're doing to generate publicity and get the public concerned about it. But, in the end, nothing can happen without the money."

"I hear you," Matt said. He was still sulking but beginning to come around.

"I'm not trying to discourage you, Matthew," Eleanor told him. "I still believe we're going to save this forest in the end."

"Me too," Matt said positively.

"That's why we're working with these other agencies, like the Land Trust and the Watershed Association. These are agencies that can generate awareness and raise the necessary funds. It's business, this thing. Trent Development Company bought this land for a certain amount of money and they're going to make a profit on it somehow. We have to offer them at least slightly more than they bought the land for, if not close to what they speculate they can make off the condo sales. It's big money. Right now, the land is theirs. They can do whatever they want with it. We have to make them *want* to look noble for preserving the land, while in reality what they're doing is settling for less of a profit than they were banking on in the first place."

Matt grinned again. "Or less of a hassle to cut their losses and get out of town."

"True," said Eleanor. "Will you be all right, now?"

Matt shrugged it off, letting his true alpha male side shine through. "I'm fine," he said, straightening up.

"Good," Eleanor said. She continued down the steps with her gentle, certain footsteps, looking down as she went. "You did a fine job tonight. Don't concern yourself with feeling bad about it."

"Thank you," he said. "I won't."

CHAPTER 16

Matt strode up to the main entrance of the Northeast Water Treatment Plant, trying desperately to shake his feelings of foolishness and uncertainty. The outfit wasn't helping. It was the first time in years that he'd thrown on a blazer, and his shoulders and waistline had both plumped since then. He couldn't quite get all three buttons done, so he left it open to show off his new 100% recycled cotton tie and pressed white shirt. His khakis were ironed and he wore the same pair of dress shoes that he wore to Pete Schola's funeral, which was over fifteen years ago, now. He should have just rolled up in his chaps and his work boots, same as always. Maybe he would have felt a little underdressed around the president in a get-up like that, but it would have been better than what he was feeling now. He tugged at the tight knot in his tie, the same way he did on his way into church for first communion.

He had an orange plastic badge pinned to the breast of his blue blazer that read: *Press/ Guest* next to a black and white printout of the presidential seal. At the bottom it read: *Arborist Matthew Largess.* Under his arm he held a file folder filled with information about Oakland Forest. He had aerial photographs, pictures taken from the forest floor, charts and graphs showing the statistics about old growth forests and how they applied to Oakland forest, the results from the University of Rhode Island testing, letters from the Watershed Association and the Land Trust, newspaper clippings… everything. There was even a nice calendar with a different old growth forest around the nation for every month of the year, and a little pamphlet entitled *Voice of the Forest* describing his credentials, his role in the effort and the prophecy of Crystal Powers. He and Eleanor put it all together (She was the one who arranged this meeting). After seeing this, there was no way the president was going to be able to forget about it. This was his type of thing; he was an environmental guy.

At the entrance he was greeted by two nondescript secret service agents who guarded the door. They had the sunglasses and the ear-pieces and the whole bit. The two stepped in front of Matt's path at the door in unison. One of them reached out and inspected the badge pinned to his breast, and then held his arm out towards the door.

"Take the stairs to the second level. An agent will meet you there to take you to him," he said.

"Mmmhmm," Matt replied.

He stepped through the heavy glass doors of the foyer and stood in the lobby of the treatment plant. It was a tall, open building with steep, cast iron staircases and iron railings that rose up six stories high. There were all sorts of holding tanks, ducts and pipes winding their way everywhere. It was an old building that had tried to keep up with the times by adding new equipment right on top of, or next to the old in an effort to cut costs. The end result was the maze of tubes and tanks that Matt peered up into from the lobby floor.

He heard the sound of children's laughter echoing through the building and looked up to see if he could locate it. Then, following the laughter he heard the soft, leathery smooth southern tones of the man himself. There was no mistaking it. Talk about snake oil salesmen! He was about to meet the number one snake-oiler of all time. One earfull of that voice pouring out at you and you were ready to sign your life away on the dotted line.

Matt grinned and walked to the bottom of the staircase where another secret service agent waited to inspect his badge. The man clicked the button on his two-way radio and spoke monotonously, "I have Arborist Matthew Largess, here."

The radio clicked to life. "Affirmative," spoke a voice eerily similar to the man standing before him. "Send him up."

"The president will see you now," said the agent. "Go up two flights. He's with a class of second-graders."

"Mmmhmm!" said Matt. He lowered his big bald head and stomped up the stairs, hearing the voices get closer and more distinct until he arrived on the third level and saw him standing there in the midst of the children. A middle-aged woman, presumably the schoolteacher, stood looking on slightly away from the pack. The president was flanked by two more secret service agents that hovered close by.

There he was, no more than twenty feet away from him. Matt stood there, frozen, staring at him.

President Clinton stood tall in front of the kids with his hands clasped in front of him, smiling and listening to their questions. They were all in the large open walkway, close to the railing on the open side of the building, away from the bulk of the tanks and tubes. Clinton saw Matt standing there gawking at him and waved him over.

"Mr. Largess!" he called out. "Come on over. Don't be shy, now."

"Hi!" Matt said, and felt awkward for the way it came out. He took a breath and started walking towards him.

"Now kids, this is a man who's trying to save a forest right around where you live, isn't that right?"

The kids, who'd all been staring with infatuation at Clinton, shifted their heads all at once to hear Matt's response.

"That's right," Matt confirmed. "I..." For one of the first times in his life, he opened his mouth and nothing came out. He, too was caught up in the spell. He just looked so good standing there, in his perfectly tailored suit, his power tie and his flawless shimmering gray hair. And his eyes had the same quality as Matt's own did. They had that extra shimmering behind them; that spark of life that overflowed with charisma.

"Come right on over and let me shake your hand," said the President. He held his hand out towards Matt. "Kids, if you would be so kind as to step aside to let Mr. Largess through."

The kids shuffled aside and stared at Matt, who stepped through and grasped onto Clinton's hand.

Clinton took it and then clasped his other hand over the top, giving him the old two-hander. "I want you to know that I appreciate everything you're doing. The environment is the number one issue in this country right now, and not everyone understands that. If we want this world to be a better place for our kids," he said, removing one of his hands to gesture towards the children. "Kids, it's men like Mr. Largess, here, that are the true heroes of this country."

The kids turned their heads up to Matt again and looked at him curiously, as if they were thinking, *but we thought you were the hero, Mr. President.*

"Mmmhmm!" Matt started. "Well... thank you Mr. President. But... I really haven't done anything yet. I mean, I'm trying but I'm not sure if it's gonna work out. They could be over there with bulldozers tomorrow, for all I know."

"You can't think that. You can't give up," Clinton said earnestly.

"No. I won't," Matt assured him.

"Now, what's the name of this place? It's Oakland Forest, isn't it?"

"Yeah," said Matt, emboldened by the fact that the President remembered the name. "Hey! You know what we should do? You should hop in my truck and we can take a ride over there right now. We can be there in twenty minutes. You have to see this place. It's magical. I feel like if you just went there, you'd understand."

Clinton smiled and clapped Matt on the shoulder. "There's nothing I'd enjoy more than getting in your truck with you right now and going for a ride. But that's one of the drawbacks of the job," he said, and flashed his narrow-eyed smile. "You're my 10:57 this morning. I'm meeting someone else at 11:04."

"Oh," Matt said, disappointed. "Mmmhmm. I gotcha."

"But rest assured I'll remember this little talk we had here, today. I'm not so busy that I can't remember the things that matter most."

"Wow! Really?"

"Absolutely. I told you how I feel about the environment. It was a pleasure, Mr. Largess," Clinton said. He gave him a slight nod and then looked away, placing both hands on the railing and staring out into the plant.

Matt felt a hand on his shoulder and turned to see the secret service guy standing right behind him.

"Oh... likewise," he said, and followed the agent away. "Have a great day," he added over his shoulder.

Matt barely even remembered walking out of the building. It was like he was floating on air, sauntering his way through some kind of dream world in which he'd just been commended by the President of the United States. The next thing he knew, he was sitting in his truck, staring blankly out the windshield. Everything he looked at had a soft, warm glow about it. That is, until he caught sight of the file folder resting on his thigh.

That snake-oiler! How was he supposed to *think* while that guy was running his mouth? It was like hypnotism!

He had to get back there and get him this folder. Everything depended on it. If he didn't get it... this whole thing was a waste of time!

Matt burst out of his truck and bounded through the parking lot up to the main entrance. His shoes pinched at him and his khakis threatened to tear open at the crotch, but nothing slowed him. He got to the door all red in the face, fully out of breath and halted before the agent.

"I have to... get this to.. the president," he stammered in between breaths. "It's... important."

The agent crossed his arms in front of his chest. "You're time is up, Mr. Largess. I'm afraid I can't let you back in for security purposes."

"What!" Matt roared. "What am I gonna do? I need to give him these papers!"

"Mr. Largess. Step away from me. You're threatening me," said the agent, coldly.

Matt took a half step backwards. "No, I'm not."

"I'm going to need you to leave the premises immediately. Don't make me press this button and make a show out of it." He had his hand on the button for his two-way radio.

Matt slumped his shoulders. He looked into the dark sunglasses of the agent and saw there was no way he could win.

"Mmmhmm," Matt said, turning away. "I've been hearing that more and more, lately."

CHAPTER 17

I saw Matt one afternoon in August. It was during a hot, dry spell when the lawns were all dried up and dust rose up off the ground with every step. I had been working at his place, building a stone retaining wall in his backyard. Matt saved me with the work, really, because I had nothing else going on at the time. He lived in an electric-blue painted raised ranch on the north shore of Jamestown, inland a ways and on top of the highest hill on the island. It was a big, triple lot with piles of firewood (half of it rotted) and sailing gear stacked up all over the yard. He came out on fire, as usual. He must have seen my truck pull up and he came storming out of the house at me, with his massive bald head leaning out in front of him and his arms and legs chugging away to keep up. It was like his whole body was being pulled forward by the sheer force in those crazy eyes.

"What's up, Daddy? How's it going?" he boomed out cheerfully.

My wife had given birth to a beautiful baby girl, Vivian, just a few weeks earlier. It was amazing. That, understandably, was all I was really concerned about at the time. Being with my wife in the delivery room and seeing her pump my little baby girl out had given me a whole new respect for her. My girl was tough, and she'd baked up the perfect little tiny human, complete with all the necessary innards and extremities. All I cared about was them. Throw in the sleep deprivation along with the wonderment of the whole thing and it was like I was walking around in my own little bubble with no real correlation to what was going on in the real world.

"Pretty good," I said, trying to rub some of that bubble-haze out of my eyes. "How's it going with you?"

"Good. I owe you some money."

"True," I said.

"Is it okay if I give you 500 and another 500 next week?"

"Yeah. That's fine."

"Are you sure?" he asked.

He always asked me that when he owed me money. He always paid me, and always in a timely manner. I wondered how he'd respond if I busted his balls and told him, "No. Give it all to me right now or things are gonna get awfully physical around here." But then again, I knew he could destroy me if it really came down to it. He had freakish brute strength and was arguably insane; a hellish combo. So I let it go.

"Yeah," I said. "That's cool."

"Come on inside," he said.

I followed him in and downstairs into his office. It was nice and air-conditioned down there. I could feel the cool creeping over my sweaty, dusty skin as I walked in. Then, standing in the threshold, I was stunned to find the place looking relatively neat and orderly. When I first met him there was junk everywhere down there. There were books, tools, laundry (clean *and* soiled), sailing gear, and tons of those random sheets of computer paper everywhere, even more than there were upstairs.

"What the hell happened down here?" I asked.

"You like what Anna's done with the place?"

"Who?"

"Anna. I hired a high school girl to come in and straighten me out. She's great. She just finds a place for everything and then tells me where it is. I have to get more on top of it. I'm losing stuff, missing payments… all that."

"Well, it looks great," I said.

"Yeah. Look at this place." Matt sat down at his desk on one of his wheeled computer chairs and took out his big check ledger. I took a seat at the chair in front of his computer, which was on a separate desk on the adjacent wall.

"Unbelievable, isn't it?" he continued. "So I'll give you five now, check, and then I'll give you five cash at the end of the week. Pay-pay. And that's fine. Then I'll be all caught up on the wall and we can get going to the next thing. The next thing. What are we gonna do next?"

"I don't know," I said. "Whatever you want. We'll figure it out."

"Yeah. You sure it's fine? I'm not getting too behind, am I? I'm keeping you greased with pay-pay pretty good?"

"Yeah. It's perfect."

Matt sighed and took out his checkbook. "This fucking thing. Cash cow. Milk me, milk me! Squirt- squirt! Ha! How do I spell your name, again? I ask you this every time. I don't know why I don't get it. Maybe it's cause I'm dislexic. What is it? F-l-a-…r?"

"No. There's a "her" in the middle. Lots of micks do it like that." And I spelled it out for him, the whole thing.

"e-y?" he asked.

"No. T- Y. F-l-a-h-e-r-T-y. Are you really dislexic, or are you just saying that?"

"No, man. I am. I have serious learning disabilities, dude. Some of this stuff is really hard for me. Writing checks… writing… that's why I need you to be the writer."

"Really?" I asked. "I never would have guessed. Do your kids have it, too?"

"No. Just me. I think I'm… what's that word when people are really smart at one thing and they can't do normal things like other people?"

"Autistic?" I ventured.

"Yeah. I'm special, man. Like Rainman. Trees, forestry… I get really into it like no one regular ever could. But when it comes to papers, letters and numbers, I'm no good. You saw this office before, didn't you?"

"Yeah," I said.

"I think I'm going up to Moosehead Lake next week, midweek, I think. I'm just gonna go up there and get in there… deep."

"Nice," I said.

The phone rang.

"Stay down here for a minute. Take a break. It's too hot," he said.

I hadn't worked a lick yet all day. I was still in my flip-flops, and it was 11:30. I had been dicking around, half-hungover, playing guitar to my little girl all morning. "Sure," I said.

The phone conversation was all about sailing, making travel plans for getting to a regatta, until Matt spun it with an out-of-nowhere comment about black bears and their natural habitat and about the trees in Maine. He was rambling on for a good minute about it.

Matt laughed and hung up the phone. "He hung up on me. He thinks I'm crazy. See?"

"See what?" I asked.

"No one wants to fucking listen. But I don't care. I keep talking. Keep going 'til someone listens. That's *your* problem!"

I laughed at him. "What's my problem?"

"You get all sad because people won't read your books. Because none of the publisher shitheads will listen to you. Now you stopped talking. You can't do that. You're letting them win. You have to keep talking. You're too sensitive."

"You think I'm sensitive, you should see other writers. They make me look—"

Matt wasn't listening to anything I was saying. It was too late. He was zoned in. "It's like the Friars, or the Celtics," he went on. "What are you gonna do when you're down twenty at half-time? You gonna quit or go out there and play the second half?"

"Fight," I said, patronizing him now. "Go out there and scrap for it. Never say die."

"Damn right! You wait. Wait 'til the book comes out! I'd like to see them make me shut up! I'm telling you, this book is gonna be huge. This is the one that's gonna break you. And me! No one can shut me up! Do you believe it?"

"Yeah," I said, laughing.

"Bullshit," he said, frowning. "You don't believe it. But you better, or it's not even worth doing."

"Now, when you say *the book*, you're referring to the one you think I'm writing about you?"

"What do you mean, *think?*"

I looked at him and figured it would crush him if I told him that I hadn't written a word yet, and that I didn't plan on writing it. I thought about lying to him just to keep his spirits up. But then I'd have a lot of explaining to do, later. I had to let him have it, now.

"Matt," I said. "I want to be very clear about this. I'm not writing a book about you. Okay?"

He frowned and crossed his arms over his chest. "Bullshit," he said.

I laughed. "What do you mean? I'm telling you, it's not gonna happen."

"Oh yeah?" he retorted, incredulously. "Did I tell you what happened with the blessings?"

"Yeah. I was there with you, remember? Poof! Gone," I said.

"No, that was the *first* one," he said. His eyes got wide, and he smiled and leaned forward in his chair. "Now there have been *three*. And every single one of them has happened like that. Now are you gonna tell me it was the wind that blew them away?"

I shrugged. "Maybe," I said.

"Shame! Shame!" he said loudly, leaning back with his head raised towards the ceiling.

He said this more to tease me than because he was getting upset with me. It was a good sign. I liked when he got like this. It usually meant he was going to be able to handle whatever I said to him; that he wasn't going to get flipped on one of his trademark split-second mood changes.

"You're just saying that because you don't want to believe it. Because you don't want to write it. I see what you are, now. You're just lazy. You don't want to write it because it's too much work. You just want to get drunk and smoke your weed and play guitar all day, or write stupid shit that isn't hard because it's all weird and artistic. You don't want to write anything that means anything because it's too hard. I see how it is. You're *that* kind of hippie. I thought you were the kind who cared about the earth and believed in spiritual stuff. My mistake."

"Whatever," I said. "I'm running an all-organic landscaping business. And you think I'm lazy? I built you a fucking stone wall in a week. I've written two books and I'm only twenty-six."

"Yeah, but they're not any good. They don't sell."

"Oh," I said. I laughed it off but inside I was really pissed. "Now the fangs come out."

"Hey," he said. "The numbers don't lie, man. You're a good writer, you just don't write about the right thing. You write my story, and it'll sell. *I'll* sell it. I met the president the other day, a couple weeks ago. He loves me."

I was ready to fire another one back at him until I realized what he'd just said. "The president?" I asked.

He showed me a cocky smirk and nodded his head affirmatively.

"You mean, like the President of the United States of America, *that* president?"

"Mmmhmm. Slick Willy. He told me I was a hero. He told me the environment is the number one issue in the world today, and that's what I'm fighting for. You still think it's not a good enough story?"

"Clinton?" I asked.

"I sent a copy of one of those blessings to Julia Butterfly Hill. Someone in her inner circle wrote me back and asked me not to send another one. He said she came undone when she laid her eyes on it."

I still didn't know who Julia Butterfly Hill was. "Inner circle?" I started. "What do you mean, she came *undone?*"

"He said she lost it. Said she started going crazy and babbling and couldn't settle down all night. *That's* how powerful it is. I'm telling you, man. It's real. You still don't believe me?"

I laughed uncomfortably. "I don't know," I said.

Matt saw he was making me uncomfortable and it gave him more energy. He liked this. I had noticed that about him, by now. Whenever he saw that someone was looking at him like he was crazy, he'd hit them with another couple comments that were even further out-there before he reeled them back in.

"Yeah! Mmmhmmm! And we have to have a chapter about the ivory-billed woodpecker. Did I tell you I want to go down to Arkansas to find it? No one can get a picture of it but it's because they're not looking in the right place. Or because the bird doesn't want them to. I think it wants me. I think I'm the one."

I wasn't going to let him get me with his tricks. "Why would I write a chapter about some freekin' woodpecker if I was writing a book about how you're trying to save the forest. It doesn't have anything to do with the story."

"Yes! Yes, it does!" He pounded his fist on the table, up-ending a coffee mug full of pens. "It has everything to do with the story! It's all connected!"

The foam was forming in the corner of his mouth and he rolled a few inches closer to me in his office chair.

"Get away from me," I said, laughing. I pushed myself a few feet away from him, towards the door.

"Wait a minute! Does that mean you're gonna write it, now? You're already making plans for the chapters!"

"No."

"You know what else we have to have? We have to have the story of my recovery in there. And I want all the old shit… the drugs, the booze, the whores… everything. 'Cause that's all part of what makes me like this. Now I don't have that stuff to obsess about, so I need something else. That's how my brain works. That's why I can put all this energy into the forest. You see how it works?"

I was surprised by what perfect sense he was making. "Yeah," I said sincerely.

"See? I'm telling you. This forest is going to be saved. There's no way it can happen any other way. I believe that, now. I'm the chosen one… the voice of the forest."

I snorted at him. "Last week you said it didn't look good. You were all down in the dumps."

He sighed. "That was a low moment," he admitted. "It's hard. It takes a lot out of me, sometimes."

I felt bad for him, then. I was about to say something to cheer him up when he snapped his head up and his eyes came alive again.

"So, how about those Celts? What do you think about their draft picks? What's the name of that high school guy they got?"

"Jesus Christ," I said. "Is that where we're going, now? I have to go get some work done."

I stood up out of my seat and made a move for the door.

"Hey! Don't point your finger at me! I'm not the one walking around in his flip-flops at noon! You lazy hippie!"

I kept going. I could hear him chuckling behind me while I walked up his basement stairs to get outside. He thought he was really getting me good.

"Yeah? Keep it up. I'll *never* write your stupid book," I said over my shoulder.

"You will!" he roared.

I heard him thunder up the stairs and clatter against the screen door while I headed down the new walkway (that I'd just installed a week earlier) out to my truck.

"After this forest gets saved you'll be begging me to write this book! And then maybe I'll get a different writer!"

"Go ahead," I told him.

"Yeah. Mmmhmm," he said softly, his mind already spinning off on another tangent. "Walkway looks good," he muttered, and disappeared into the house.

CHAPTER 18

Matt stood in the midst of a hundred Monica Lewinski look-a-likes at the Newport Airfield, pressing to fight his way to the very front of the roped-off area set back from the runway. It was during the height of the *"I did not have relations with that woman"* scandal, and the undergrads from Salve Regina University and URI all came out to protest in the form of black wigs, sunglasses, lipstick, over-stuffed bras and business-skirts. There were Monicas sprinkled throughout the crowd of five hundred or so that were there to greet the President, the most enthusiastic of which had pushed their way up to the front to give him a good look the moment he stepped off the plane.

Matt was dripping sweat in the August heat underneath his blue blazer and khaki pants, the same get-up he'd worn to meet President Clinton a few weeks before. He clung tightly to the folder he'd forgotten to hand him, containing the glossy photographs of the forest and the scientific documents supporting his claims. The little orange *Press/ Guest* pass was still pinned to his breast. Thank God for that pass. That pass was the inspiration and the backbone behind his whole plan.

He was almost to the front of the crowd. There was a walkway roped off that cut through the center of the crowd, leading up to a black limousine about a hundred yards back. All that stood between him and a prime front row position were three rows of Lewinskis. There was a rumble through the crowd and people pointed up at the sky as the humming of a jet engine came into earshot. Some even leaned in to the crowd to try and inch their way closer, being drawn in by the aura and mystique of laying eyes on the President of our country.

Matt took it to a whole new level. He reached his arm in between two Lewinskis, bellowed, "Press!" and plowed right through them.

"Watch it, pervert!" one of the girls snapped at him, straightening her jet black wig that Matt had jostled down over her eyes.

"Hey! How do you know I'm a pervert? I'm a member of the press. Out of the way! Important press business! I'm a photographer for the Boston Globe! I need to get up front!"

"Where's your camera?" the girl asked.

Matt looked away from her and straight-armed his way through two more disapproving Lewinskis. "Out of the way! Press! Reporter!" he hollered. Only one more push. This time he used two hands and shoved both the girls in the front row by their shoulders, clearing space for his wide frame and announced "I'm sorry. Important press business. I need this front row. I'm sorry."

The girls sneered at him through their dark sunglasses and red lipstick. As Matt turned away to look for the plane he was greeted by more sunglasses boring in on him, this time belonging to two secret service agents who had marched over to see what all the commotion was.

"Press," Matt said weakly, and pointed to the laminated badge on his breast.

The two suits looked him up and down, frowned, and then turned their back to him.

The jet touched down on the runway with a puff of smoke from the tires and a rise of applause from the crowd. Once it got to the end of the runway and slowed to a reasonable driving speed it wheeled its way around in a wide arc and headed for the reception area. The commotion and applause died down a bit in waiting while the big metal stairs were rolled up to the door and then rose to a crescendo when the cabin door opened. Out came two more secret servicemen, followed by President Clinton and the First Lady, who held hands and raised them over their heads to salute the crowd.

Upon first glimpse of Clinton the crowd noise went berserk.

"Boo! Boo! Womanizer!" shouted the Monica closest to Matt.

"Rapist!" screamed another.

The boos rose up to battle the cheers, and then the cheers got stronger to counter the boos. It was a tug-of-war of words.

The President and Hillary Clinton sauntered toward the noise unaffected with plastic smiles, as if they were being greeted by a chorus of songbirds in springtime.

Matt's heart was pounding in his chest and his hands were trembling. *Not yet,* he told himself. *Wait for it. Wait until he gets closer.*

The Lewinskis were emboldened by the opposition of the applause. Most of them were laughing, screaming at the president more for entertainment than from real conviction.

A gray-haired man of about sixty burst through the crowd to get close to the Lewinskis gathered around Matt. He was all red in the face, screaming, "Stop that! Stop that! You should be ashamed of yourselves! This is the president of our nation!"

"Beat it, old man!" retorted the Lewinskis. "Yeah! Save it, grandpa!"

Wait for it! Matt scolded himself. *He's still too far away. Wait for it!*

But despite his warnings, Matt couldn't hold it any longer. The adrenaline and the commotion from the crowd set his body into motion even when his mind was telling him no. Matt raised his folder up over his head and leaned as far as he could over the rope. "Mr. President!" he screamed. "It's me! Matt Largess! Mr. President!"

The President was still a good ten feet away, shaking hands with someone in the front row on the other side of the aisle.

The two secret servicemen stepped swiftly in front of Matt.

"Sir! Calm down and step back!" commanded one of them.

"I'm sorry," Matt said. "I can't. It's important. I have to talk to him."

"Sir! That's not possible. Step BACK!"

The agent put a hand on Matt's chest and Matt instinctively brushed it away.

"That's it! You're under arrest!" shouted the agent.

He grabbed Matt's arm and twisted it behind him in a submission hold, causing the folder to fall and the papers within to drop and flutter around on the ground. The President's impeccably polished black shoes nearly stepped on one of them.

"Mr. President! It's me! Matt Largess! From the other day! Please!" Matt screamed as both of the agents were restraining him and reaching for their handcuffs.

The President looked over in confusion for a moment before he recognized him. "Mr. Largess," he said with his trademark tone of southern politeness. "Good to see you." He gestured for the secret servicemen to let him go. "It's all right," he said.

Upon instruction they let him go. Matt bent down and quickly scooped up the loose documents and stuffed them back in his folder.

"Thanks," said Matt, still out of breath from the struggle. He wiped the foam from the corner of his mouth and spoke frantically. "I'm sorry. It's just... I have to give you this folder... about Oakland Forest. I had it the other day and I forget to give it to you. It's important."

The First Lady was looking at him like she was genuinely afraid.

"Hi. Matt Largess," Matt said to her, and got no response.

"You have something you'd like to give me?" asked President Clinton.

"Oh! Yeah! Mmmhmmm!" Matt said, and held out the folder. "It's all about the forest I'm trying to save. You can see it from the plane, probably, when you fly over. Look down. It's the only big stand of woods just north of here... if you're flying north... I don't know."

The President accepted the folder and handed it to a member of his entourage who Matt didn't recognize. "Thank you, Mr. Largess. I'll look it over on the plane on the way home, as you suggested," he said with a warm smile, and continued down the aisle.

The two secret servicemen stepped away from Matt, straightening their ties and suit coats.

"See? We're buddies. What's your problem?" Matt said with a smirk, gloating.

CHAPTER 19

My wife Courtney and I decided to take our new baby, Vivian, on a little nature hike one Sunday afternoon. Of course I'd told her all about Matt and his mission to save the "magic" forest. She liked hearing the stories and had even met Matt a couple times, so she was curious to see the place. It wasn't very far away, so we figured it was as good a place as any to get outside for a little while. Besides that, she said it would be good for me to see that I could have fun doing things that didn't involve beers or loud rock n' roll. I couldn't see how walking through the woods could be as fun as slamming beers in a pile of manure somewhere with AC/DC blasting, but I realized this was a personal problem. She had a good point.

Vivian was cute. She still had kind of a wrinkled-up baby face from being so new but I was starting to be able to see her features poking through. She looked just like me from the nose down and had big beautiful eyes instead of my squinty ones, and they were still bright blue. I don't know where she got them from but they were beautiful.

She had her eyes closed and was sleeping inside her little sling that was wrapped around Courtney's shoulder as we walked through the path in the meadow that led into the forest. My wife is really pretty, if I do say so myself. At times I look at myself in the mirror and wonder how and why she ever took an interest in me. She's as tall as me and skinny and her waist starts about six inches higher than mine. She's got nice long legs, long arms, long blonde-brown hair and a slender pretty face.

She was just starting to be able to get around pretty good again after delivering Vivian, and I wondered if this was going to be too much for her. I put my arm around her and asked how she was feeling.

"All right," she said, and gave me a kiss on the cheek. "This sling is pulling at my neck a little, though."

"You want me carry her?" I asked.

"I don't want to wake her up," she said. "You don't think it's going to start raining on us, do you?"

I looked up at the gray sky. It was September and the air had just started to cool down again. The tall summer weeds in the meadow were burnt and bent over from the hot August sun, and the meadow grasses were reaching their full height with the flower-heads poking up from the masses.

"I don't think so," I said. "It's been like this all day."

I kept my arm around her while we walked a little while in silence.

"I like it out here," she said. "I can see why Matt wants to save it. See? This is fun, isn't it?"

"Yeah," I agreed. "I like breaking the law. Adds a little something to the experience," I said, and was immediately sorry I said it.

"What do you mean?" asked Courtney, nervously. She didn't like doing things she wasn't supposed to. She's a good girl.

"Nothing. I'm just kidding. I'm sorry. I just said it because I knew it would make you nervous. I'm a jerk."

"You are a jerk. Are we not supposed to be here or something?"

Technically, the forest belonged to the development company and we were trespassing but Courtney didn't need to know that. "No," I told her. "Matt has a restraining order against him so he can't come here, but there's nothing wrong with *us* being here."

"Lovely," she said.

"Isn't it? *Restraining order* always has such a distinct ring to it. Really livens up a conversation."

We walked along slowly until we came to the boards laid across the stream that led into the forest. The water had risen since the last time I was here, and the footing around the bank was muddy and slippery. I held out my arm to steady her and we crossed over the stream.

"Don't drop the baby in the river," I said.

"That wouldn't be good," she said, giggling.

When we got to the other side she asked me to take a picture of her and the baby. She had her nice camera with her, the big old one with the long lens. I didn't know much about cameras but Courtney did. And I knew she liked this one the best, better than the other two digital ones she had that self-focused. This was the kind where you had to twist the big lens and then bring the film in to get developed and everything. I was always getting scolded for half-assing it and not getting the picture in good focus before I took the shot.

Courtney handed me the camera and pulled back the flap of the sling just a bit so I could see a peek of Vivian's face. I raised the thing up, told her to smile, twisted the lens into focus and snapped the shot. Then I took another one, this time with the flash on.

"Did you get it good?" she asked.

"I think so. Probably not," I said.

"Shame, C'mon," she complained. "We don't have any good pictures of me and we have a million of you."

"I think I got it good," I protested. "I think I'm starting to like this one."

I handed the camera back to her and we started walking along the path in the forest, underneath the high canopy of the beech branches. There was very little wind and it was really quiet in there.

"It feels cooler in here," Courtney said.

"I know. Even though there isn't any sun for the leaves to shade us out from. It's like the ground is cooler in here, or something."

"Yeah," she said, and started giggling again. "It must be part of the magic. The leaves turn into magic pixie dust on the ground when they rot."

"Sshh!" I scolded her. "Don't upset the spirits within."

"Shame! Don't say that! Why would you say that? That's freaky!"

"Hey! You started it," I said. "You can see forever in here, huh?"

"Yeah," she said. "All I can see is trees. I thought you said you could see houses in here."

"You can," I told her. I squinted through the tree trunks until I found one off in the distance and pointed it out to her. "And you remember how we parked right next to a neighborhood on the other side."

"You're right," she said, tilting her head back to look up at the trees. "The trees aren't that big. How old did he say they are?"

"One million years old. Before the dawn of time."

"No. *Really,*" she said.

"I don't know. Two or three hundred, I think."

"So… do you believe him or not? Because sometimes you sound like you do and sometimes you sound like you don't."

"Today? No. Ever since I came here with him that day, I don't think so. I'm not saying it's impossible, I just don't think so. I don't blame him for saying whatever he can to try and save the place. It's nice in here… worth saving."

"But didn't he get tests from scientists and stuff?"

"That's what he said. But he's a bullshit artist. A self-proclaimed snake-oil salesman. You know that."

"Yeah," she said. "He's nice, though."

"He's a great guy. He's a piece of work. I'm gonna go trudge around off the beaten path for a minute. I want to see if I can find some of the big White Oaks he's talking about. I bet there's nothing bigger than the one in our yard. That thing's a whopper," I said. I started stomping through the deep leaf litter towards some thicker trees that I saw set back a little ways.

"All right," she said. "Don't go too far."

"Why? You scared?" I called back.

"No," she said tentatively. "Yes. We're out here all alone."

"I know. I'm not going far," I said.

I had only walked about fifty yards when I heard a branch snap a few feet behind me. I started laughing, thinking that Courtney was too scared to stay away from me. "What's the matter?" I asked, turning my head. "You—"

Only she wasn't standing beside me where the noise came from. She was back on the path, fiddling with her camera. And now she was laughing at me. "Somebody over there with you?" she asked. Then she put her hands up by her face, twinkled her fingers, and made a pathetic *Moo-ha-ha-ha* raspy call that sounded like it was straight off the set of a bad 1960's vampire movie.

I was about to snap back at her when I heard a loud bang and an echoing crack coming from the perimeter of the forest, seemingly in the direction of the neighborhood on the other side. I couldn't be sure, but it sounded like a gunshot to me. I froze for an instant and then started walking back to my wife in a hurry.

"Hey!" I yelled out as loud as I could. "Cut the shit! We're humans in here! Humans!"

Courtney was dying laughing now, trying to get her camera up to get a picture of me running scared. "Rats!" she said as I came up to her, still laughing.

"You're going to wake the baby up, laughing like that," I said.

"You should have seen your face. What the hell? I can't get my camera to work. It just made this weird noise and shut off and I can't turn it back on. What the hell?" Now she was getting frustrated with her expensive camera and smacking it with the palm of her hand.

Then we heard the crack three times in quick succession. There was no doubt in my mind this time. They were gunshots.

"What is that? Is that a gun?" she asked.

"I think so."

"So! Don't just stand there! Yell!"

So then we were both standing there in the middle of the woods, screaming. "Humans! Humans! Don't shoot us!"

The shots kept going off one after the other and we finally realized they were pretty far away and we were being ridiculous. We laughed about it.

"Maybe there's a shooting range over there, or something," Courtney suggested.

"Maybe," I said, relieved. "It's weird, though. Seems like it's just a rich people's neighborhood over there. Maybe some freekin' nut-job has a firing range in his backyard or something."

In a moment the firing stopped and we were left again with just the silence of the forest. It was silent and completely still for a second before the wind picked up. It started with a small rustling of leaves and built up over the course of thirty seconds or so into a stiff gust, culminating with a rise of leaves that were sent skyward from the ground in a mini-tornado in the midst of a thick cluster of beeches.

The gust subsided even quicker than it came on, all the way back down to a dead calm. The cluster of leaves fluttered back down to the ground and landed gently. I realized that I was clinging to my wife more than she was clinging to me. I reminded myself to be a man. I straightened up and rubbed her back.

"That was quite a show, huh?"

Courtney had given up trying to laugh it off. "I don't like it," she said.

There was a commotion in the brambles and the small amount of brush that bordered the stream, further along down the meadow from the entry towards the far end of the forest. We watched and listened to the squawking as what must have been two hundred tiny, jet-black birds took off from the bushes and darted into the sky.

"This is crazy," Courtney said.

Vivian stirred in her sling for the first time. She made little cooing sounds and worked her lips on an imaginary breast before nuzzling back down and going back to sleep.

"Little Viv doesn't seem to mind it," I said.

"You can't tell me you're not a little freaked out right now," she said.

"You're right. I'd say now is as good of a time as any to get out of here."

We turned around and started heading back through the woods towards our car. Courtney was holding onto my hand with a white-knuckle grip.

"If I could run I would seriously run out of here right now," she said. "I'm still too sore."

"You want me to carry the two of you?" I asked.

I heard an electronic wheeze come from her camera. She looked down at it.

"*Now* it's back on." She focused quickly on a nearby tree and took a picture. "There's nothing wrong with it now. That is so weird."

"Moo-ha-ha-ha!" I said, mimicking her scary ghost sound from before.

"Don't even joke about it," she said. "Not 'til we're back in the car."

CHAPTER 20

There was a knock at the door. Matt was down loading chunks of Norway Maple into the big wood stove in his basement.

"Come in!" he shouted, and went to work with the poker, stirring up the hot embers in the bottom of the stove. "I said '*Come in!*'."

He became annoyed after a few moments of silence, and blustered his way up the few stairs from the basement of his raised ranch that led to the front door, brushing the dust and wood shrapnel off his chest. He was wearing his old pair of navy blue overall chaps with a maroon thermal undershirt underneath. His hair stuck out in white tufts at the side and his bald head had a dull sheen to it from wearing his dirty winter hat. "Damn it," he mumbled in the direction of the front door. "It's always open. Just come in. Everyone just comes in."

Matt flung the door open, ready to burst into a lecture, to find Eleanor Higgins standing on his front stoop.

"Oh! Hey! Hi! Eleanor!" Matt said. "What the heck—"

Mat stopped short when he realized how sad she looked. He'd never seen her like this before. Her eyes, that were usually so soft and comforting, were pink and irritated. Her nose was red-tipped. And she wore a long black wool overcoat that hung down to her boot-tops. She looked like she was in mourning.

"Hello Matthew," she said weakly.

"Hey," Matt said. "What's the matter?"

Eleanor shook her head and looked away.

"Mmmhmm. It's okay. Did you drive all the way here? Wow. What if I wasn't home? You want to come inside?"

She shook her head no, still not looking at him.

"Mmmhmm. Yeah. Come inside. It's okay. I just fired up the wood stove for the first time of the year last night. It's still going. Feels nice. Come on in. You drove all this way."

"I know," she said. She wiped a tear off her eye and regained her composure somewhat. "I had to come and tell you in person. There's no easy way. It's over, Matthew. The forest is lost."

"What are you talking about?"

Eleanor shook her head. "We couldn't raise the money. They're asking too much... more than they paid for it. Usually we need them to bend a little bit... usually they do. But these people won't. I'm sorry. They're going to start clearing March 15 of next year."

"No," said Matt. "They can't do that."

"Yes. They can. And they will. I'm sorry Matthew. There's nothing else I can say. There's..."

Eleanor trailed off and started to cry. Then she turned around and began walking back to her car, a ten-year-old Mercedes, parked on the street outside Matt's house.

Matt reached his arm out to stop her but found that he couldn't move. "Hey!" he called out.

He could tell from the way that her whitish blonde hair was swaying that she was shaking her head *no.*

She got in her car and took off quickly. Just like that, she was gone.

Matt took a few steps down his walkway and watched her drive down his street until she was out of sight. Then he turned around and faced his house. He was breathing heavy. His chest heaved in and out with the strain, and his breath got shorter and shorter until he was nearly hyperventilating. When he couldn't stand it anymore, he strode up to his house and ripped the storm door off its hinges, bending the metal frame and snapping the screws loose from the waterlogged doorjamb. He stood there for a moment, trembling, clutching to the door before he flung it against the big Red Maple outside his door. "FUCK! FUCK YOU!" he roared as the glass shattered and the door clattered to rest.

At that precise moment, his sixty-five-year-old neighbor, Mrs. Williams, just happened to be walking her little white kick-me dog down the street in front of Matt's house. She picked up the dog in her arms and began walking hurriedly back home.

I ran into Tim and Weeman down at the sandwich shop in town, and they told me what went down.

"He's been down in his office for two days with the door locked. I think he's been looking at porn on the internet. I'm not sure if he's slept," said Tim.

I started laughing and then thought about it. "Are you serious?" I asked.

Weeman nodded in confirmation. "Aye. He may well wank himself to death."

"We couldn't even get him to tell us where to work today. We tried to get him to come out. We're over at the shop, splitting wood."

That sounded pretty serious to me. So after I ate I got in my truck and drove over to Matt's house, despite Tim's warnings that it was probably useless.

I saw his screen door all bent up at the base of the big Red Maple. There was broken glass all around it and all over the walkway, too. I half expected to see the house turned loose like that too when I opened up the door and went inside, but everything else was in order. I heard him scuffling around down in his office, so I walked down there to see what I could do.

"Who's there?" he called through the hollow, brown-stained panel door.

"It's Shame," I said.

There was a pause for a second and then some more shuffling around and clicking of buttons.

"What do you want?"

"I don't know," I said. "I guess I just wanted to say I'm sorry about the forest."

"Mmmhmm. Thanks. Now go away. I'm busy."

"All right, dude," I said. I put a foot up on the pale blue carpeted stairs to leave, but couldn't do it. "I can't," I told him.

"What do you mean?"

"I'm worried about you. I saw Tim and Weeman. They said you've been in here for two days. Weeman said you're trying to wank yourself to death."

"Fuck Weeman!" he roared, and pounded on his desk.

"Yeah? Well… is it true?"

There was a pause. "No. Now go away. I'm fine, okay. Mmmhmm. Thanks for coming over. I'm working in here. I'm busy. I'll… talk to you later."

"Yeah? What are you working on?"

"It's… I can't talk about it."

"Okay," I said. I paced around outside the door. "Do you want me to call someone? Like… one of your sponsors or councilors or something?"

Pause. "No. I'm fine. I'm just working."

"Well… I can't leave until you open the door," I told him. "This isn't healthy. I need to know if I have to call someone or something. What does your wife think about this? Does she know?"

"She doesn't know. I haven't been in here all day. Just a lot. Mmmhmm. I've been eating… sleeping in my bed. I'm fine."

"Then come out."

"I will. Mmmhmm. But not now."

"C'mon, dude. It's shitty news… but maybe it doesn't have to be over. Maybe you just have to go hard-core. You can go put metal spikes in the trees, or build a little house in one of 'em like your friend Mrs. Butterfly. See? I found out who she is."

"I'm not putting any fucking spikes in those trees! Besides… it's over. Mmmhmm!"

"All right. Then you have to deal with it. Quit being a pussy and come out."

"You're the pussy!" he roared.

I thought I heard him laugh, and then try to stifle it.

"See? You're laughing. It's not so bad."

"No," he said, and it didn't sound like he was laughing. "It's bad. It's bad."

"Yeah," I said. "I guess you're right. But you have to come out." I took a seat in the hallway and leaned my back up against the wall. "I'm sitting down," I said. "I got time. I'm sitting here until you come out."

I sat there for about a minute before I heard him get up out of his seat and take a few steps toward the door. I thought he was going to come out, but he started talking instead. The door was so thin it was like he was standing right next to me.

"You know what I want to do right now?" he asked me, and his voice sounded stranger than I'd ever heard it. It was garbled and phlegmy.

"What?" I asked fearfully.

"I want to go downtown and drink whiskey until I throw up and sleep it off a bit. Then I want to find some coke and go up to Providence and bang some whores down on Promenade St. How's that sound?"

"That's probably not a good idea," I said.

"Shame," he said softly. "Go away. You don't know… me. You don't have to call anyone. I have a fucking phone in here. I'm talking to people."

All of a sudden I felt really bad and stupid. I got up off the floor. "Shit," I said. "I'm sorry, Matt. I—"

"It's all right. I'm glad you came over. Mmmhmm!" Then his voice returned to normal. "I got a leaf-raking job for you. In Jamestown. It's 37 Seaview. Go over and talk to the lady. Her name's Janet."

"Okay," I said. "I'm sorry."

"You don't have to be sorry. You're just trying to help. I know."

"Good," I said. "Maybe this isn't the right time… but I need to know. Do you think I can start working for you again on December first? I should be all wrapped up by then."

"Yeah!" he answered, more enthusiastically than I expected. "Mmmhmm. The operation. Round two. Good. I need you."

I chuckled to myself. He *needed* me. "All right dude, thanks. Good luck in there." I put my hand up to the door and kind of tapped on it with my fingertips, not knowing what the hell else to do, and then left him alone.

CHAPTER 21

It was hard to believe it, but another year had rolled by in my life. Here I was again, sitting next to this madman rolling down the road in the big white Largess Forestry chip-truck. It was approaching the end of the millennium and the beginning of a new one, a monumental change in the history of the world. It was supposed to be the death of the old and the rebirth of the new. I had so much big stuff happen to me in the past year, with my first daughter coming down the chute and with me starting up my own business. And now it seemed like none of it mattered. I was back, regressing into a dead-end job, getting paid 12 bucks an hour to freeze my ass off. *It's just for the winter,* I told myself. *Next year I'll have to figure out something better.*

It was the first time I'd seen Matt since we were talking to each other through the door to his office. (I guess I hadn't technically *seen* him that time, either.) He called me once a couple weeks before I was set to start to make sure we were still on, and he sounded pretty good. He told me he was doing much better and he even thanked me for coming over to check on him, which made me feel better about the whole thing. I felt like a jerk there for a while, like a stupid young kid who thinks he understands everything when in actuality he doesn't have a clue. That *is* what I was, but at least he recognized that I meant well.

"So!" Matt boomed out. "The operation! What do you think about the operation? Second time around—better or worse?"

He was driving with his red hard-hat on with the ear-protectors flipped up over his head like Mickey Mouse. He was jostling around from the shifting of the truck as we drove, and seemed to me like a big happy-go-lucky bobble-head doll. Whatever low funk he'd been in had surely lifted. This was Matt as I knew him.

"I don't know," I said. "I haven't actually worked yet. I've been sitting in your living room and driving around in the truck with you all morning."

"So? You're my writer. That's part of your job. Study. Mmmhmmm!"

"Whatever," I said. There was no use telling him I wasn't going to write it, anymore. I was surprised that he kept at it even though the dream had died, but not that surprised. He was just talking, stream of consciousness. Whatever came to the surface through the vibrations in that oversized shiny dome came out of his mouth.

"C'mon! C'mon! How do you like the operation? You love it, don't you?"

"Yes," I said. "Yes. I love it."

"Yeah! Mmmhmmm. I knew it! That's why I like having you around. You've got a great attitude."

"Yeah!" I echoed, matching his intensity just for the hell of it.

"Mmmhmm! Mmmhmm!" he stated in the direction of the windshield.

It was 9:30 and we had yet to work at all this morning. Tim and Weeman were following us in the gray one-ton dump truck. "Just out of curiosity, where are we going now?" I asked him.

"Call came in to the answering service. Lady wants a big White Oak taken down in her front yard. If it's healthy, I'm gonna save it. I'm gonna save a lot of trees, now, even more than before. That's what it's all about."

"Good," I said.

"And I'll tell you what. Guess who I got a letter from a couple weeks ago."

"President Clinton."

"No," he said, and looked at me in slight confusion. "He never gave me a letter."

"Oh."

"Crystal Powers!"

"Oh my God," I said. "That freak of nature. I still have nightmares about her. She haunts me."

"Mmmhmm! She says it's not over with the forest. She says there's still hope. She says if I stay strong that it's still gonna happen. She says it's all up to me."

"That's good."

"Yeah. What's the matter? You don't believe her?" he asked, and looked at me with grave concern.

I've always been amazed at how much Matt values my opinion. It didn't make much sense to me. I felt like I had the power to crush him or make him believe with my next words.

"I'm inclined to believe her," I told him, sparing him.

"Yeah!" he roared.

"Yeah, baby!" I told him. "She's a freak of nature! Did I ever tell you what happened to me and Courtney when we walked through there?"

"Fifty-seven!" Matt bellowed, and jacked up the brakes.

"Jesus!" I said. I looked into the side mirror and fully expected us to be rear-ended by Tim. I lost sight of him in the mirror; he was that close, but somehow he managed to stop before he smashed us.

"Let's go! Let's go!" Matt bellowed.

He was out of the truck before I could scoop my gloves up off the floor. I scrambled out and tried to catch up with him. He was already heading up the walkway to the front door. It was a ranch house with a tiny yard in a middle-class neighborhood behind the mansions in Newport. There was a huge old White Oak in the front yard, taking up the whole yard and stretching its massive limbs over the house and street. A few dark brown leaves clung to the twigs on the lower branches even though it was December.

Matt walked over to the tree, put his bare hand on the trunk, and looked up into the sprawling, sturdy limbs. He hugged the tree, pressing his cheek close against the bark.

"Look at that! I can't even get my arms around it!"

"Aye!" Weeman called out to him from the curb. "Why don't you drop your drawers and make love to it, while you're at it!"

"Shut up, Weeman!" Matt hollered, and laughed. "I'll have you deported!" Then he turned his attention back to the tree. "It's beautiful," he said, nearly whispering. "Perfectly healthy."

"You want me to gas up the saws?" I asked him. I was cold and I wanted something to do.

"No! No!" he snapped. "You come with me. I want you to see this." He leaned in and started barging towards the door. "You guys gas up the saws and get the ropes ready!" he called out to Tim and Weeman.

I shrugged my shoulders and followed a few steps behind him as he marched up the concrete steps and pounded on the door.

An older woman came to the door. She was probably in her mid-fifties and looked like she'd had a tough go of it. It could have been just the beat-up bathrobe she was wearing or the dim light emanating from the house, but that's the impression I got. She had dark eyes and deep wrinkles in her brow.

"Hi! Hey! Matt Largess, Largess Forestry at your service!"

The lady looked confused for a moment and then replied, "Oh! The tree man. Yes. I'm glad you came."

"Mmmhmmm! You called because you wanted this tree removed."

"Oh, yes," she said. "I hate that damned tree. For years I've been—"

"I'll tell you what we're gonna do," said Matt. "This is a beautiful tree. I love this tree. I'm gonna have my guys get out, climb it and prune the dead wood. Maybe trim a couple limbs that are hanging over the house just for precautionary measures. Not because it really needs it, just to make you feel better about it."

The lady's face took on a look of concern, and the deep wrinkles in her brow folded over on one another and her eyes seemed to retreat deeper into her skull. "Now, wait a minute. I don't want the tree *trimmed*. I want it *gone*. I hate that damned tree. For years I've been putting up with it and I can't stand it anymore. Stealing all of my damned light and dropping little branches on the roof."

When she said *roof* it sounded like *ruff*.

"No," said Matt. "That's not what we're gonna do. This tree is perfectly healthy. It's beautiful. It's one of the biggest White Oaks in all of Newport County."

She shook her head. "It may be beautiful to you, but it's my tree and I want it gone. If you don't want to do it, I'll call somebody else who will."

"Why? You want cancer?" Matt asked her.

The lady looked at him sideways, peeked over his shoulder to look at me, and then to Matt again. "Excuse me?" she asked.

"You want cancer? Yeah? Fine! I'll cut the tree down. This tree is like a cancer *shield*. You want the ocean coming up in your front lawn? Global warming! You only live a mile from the ocean! This tree filters out all of the toxins that are destroying the ozone layer!"

Matt had her pinned with his sparkling blue eyes. He might as well have been a cop shining a flashlight in her eyes.

She broke off eye contact and chuckled, then she looked at me.

"Is this guy for real?" she asked me.

I smiled and nodded yes.

Matt chuckled, too. "Mmmhmmm! You know who this is? This is Shamus Flaherty. He's a famous writer. He's writing a book about me because I'm a famous tree preservationist. You've probably seen me on the news. You watch the news, don't you?"

"Well... yes. But I don't recall—"

"See that? Let my guys do their work and then you can tell everybody you had a famous tree guy come in and save your tree."

The lady smiled and opened the storm door a bit more. She reached out her hand and touched Matt on the arm of his fleece jacket with her bony fingers. "I know your type," she said. "You're a charmer, aren't you. Are you trying to charm an old lady?"

"I'll tell you what we're gonna do," Matt replied. "We're going to prune off all the dead limbs—there's not many—and take off a little more to let some more light into the yard and into the house. No more little sticks dropping on the roof. Six hundred bucks. It'd cost you over two grand to have it removed. And it'll be as safe as can be. There's no *way* this tree is any kind of threat to your house. It's beautiful, completely healthy. What do you say? Is it a deal? C'mon. A deal's a deal."

The old spinster chuckled and the phlegm rattled around in her throat. "All right," she said. "I'll give it a try. If I don't like it I'll cut it down a few years from now."

"No," said Matt. "You'll see. Once we're done with this, you'll never want this tree gone. You'll love it."

The lady waved him and retreated back into the house. "I'll go get my checkbook," she said over her shoulder.

Matt stepped back and punched me on the shoulder. "See that? I'm a preservationist. We're famous. You like that? That's what I tell people, now. That's good, right?"

"You're pretty good," I conceded.

"Yeah," he said. He exhaled and puffed his chest out with pride. "I'm on fire today," he said, squinting his eyes and looking into the neighbor's yard. "That dogwood over there needs pruning. Look at that. The car's in the driveway. They're probably home. What do you think? You think I can pound on the door and get the job?"

I shrugged. "Why? Did they call you?"

He scowled at me. "No! That's not a fair bet! What do you think I am? C'mon. What do you say? What do you want to bet that I can go over there and get that job. *Blind. If* the people are home. You gotta give me that."

"Lunch," I said. "And if they call the cops on you I get a week's pay—no questions."

"They're not gonna call the cops on me. Not on the snake-oiler."

He winked at me and set out for the neighbor's house. "Timmy!" he called out en-route. "Get up in that oak and take off the dead wood and a couple limbs hanging over the house." Then he marched right up to the door and pounded on it three times—hard. I watched him work it for a couple minutes, running his mouth and waving his arms around. There was a moment's reprieve in the pitch;

during which he turned to me, gave me thumbs-up, took a bite out of an imaginary sandwich and rubbed his belly. Seconds later, he was grabbing a check from the grateful homeowner.

CHAPTER 22

The Rosecliff Mansion was boiling over with more activity that it had seen in a decade, playing host to the social elite of America on the eve of the millennium. Nearly half of the names on the *Forbes 100* list were accounted for, milling around the ballroom in shimmering gowns and tuxedoes. A twenty-five-piece big band was pumping out sounds from the last century, engaged presently in a vibrant rendition of an anthem from the roaring twenties. Caterers paraded around the room with silver trays of caviar, duck confit, steak tartar, fine wines and champagnes. At the door the guests received gold-rimmed *2000* glasses attached to a long brass rod, with the center zeroes serving as empty lenses. Many of the women had them at the ready, striking a pose whenever the opportunity afforded itself.

Eleanor Higgins was dressed in a long, elegant black gown that flowed down to the tips of her white pearl-colored heels. She wore pearls in her ears and around her neck and the whites of her eyes shimmered with the exact intensity of the pearls. Her blonde, whiting hair was sculpted and pinned back away from her eyes with a pearl-encrusted hairpin. She was involved in a conversation with some old acquaintances; an oil heiress donned in a tight red gown and bubbling with excitement, and her husband, the heir to a shoe-sole fortune. Eleanor stood there, clutching to her glass of champagne and nodding at the proper intervals, but her mind was someplace else. Behind them, she gazed out at the Atlantic ocean through the large windows that lined the entire south side of the ballroom. Past the sprawling snow-covered lawn and beneath the cliff, the dark ocean was churning in the moonlight.

Eleanor was startled to hear her cell-phone ring inside her purse. She opened it to look at her phone and found that she didn't recognize the number that was calling her. "This is strange," she said.

"Is everything all right?" asked the heiress.

Eleanor smiled. "Oh, I'm sure it is. Will you excuse me for a moment?" She began walking to the rear of the ballroom, away from the music and the crowd, and answered her phone.

"Hello?" she asked.

"Oh! Hi! Eleanor! Yeah! Hi!" Matt chimed in on the other end.

"Matthew? Is that you?"

"Yeah! Hi! Matt Largess! How are you?"

"I'm good," Eleanor said strangely. "Is everything all right?"

"Yeah! I'm great. Gr-Great!" Matt said, nearly tripping over his own words. "I just… I know this is going to sound crazy… but I think we need to go to the forest… *tonight*."

Eleanor paused and wondered if she heard him correctly. "*Tonight?*"

"Yeah! Mmmhmm! I know it sounds crazy. But… it's like… I can *feel* it. Something big's gonna happen in there tonight, I know it. It's like… I don't know how to explain it. I just know we need to go there. Crystal said only I can hear the voice of the forest and I know it, now. I don't like… hear actual voices talking to me but I just know I have to go there right away. And I need you to come with me. Something magic's gonna happen but we need to be there or it can't happen. That's what I feel."

"Matthew… it's New Year's Eve."

"I know! The eve of the millennium! Can you believe it?"

"Yes, I know. But what I'm trying to say is… I'm at a party here in Newport. I can't just… leave."

"You're in Newport! That's great!" Matt exclaimed. "Where are you? I'll come right over and pick you up! That's so great! You see? I knew it! It must be like this for a reason!"

"No," Eleanor said and sighed with frustration. "Will you just… hold on for a second please?"

She was now walking out of the ballroom, into the great marble-tiled foyer underneath the candle-lit chandelier. Eleanor stared up into the flames. All night she had been distant. She felt like something was troubling her deeply but couldn't put her finger on what it was. And now there was this strange phone call. She raised the phone back up, wondering how she could possibly be saying what she was about to say but already conceding that it would be said.

"All right," she said. "You'll need to bring me some boots."

I was sitting at home, lounging around on my couch and watching a movie when the phone rang. I figured it was one of my rowdy buddies, like Jack R. Deldon, calling to bust my balls about staying at home with my wife and kid and not coming out to party on the biggest party night in history. We couldn't get a sitter and I was pretty bummed about it at first, but now, sitting in front of the wood-burning stove with a glass of whiskey in my hand and Courtney asleep with her head resting on my lap, it didn't seem so bad. So be it. I was willing to take the heat. I got up to get the phone, stirring Courtney half-out of her sleep in the process.

"Yellow," I said, expecting to get an earful.

Instead, it was Matt. "Shame! You're home! Yeah!"

I laughed. "What do you want?"

"Why? Are you mad?" he asked.

"No," I said.

"Oh! Good. Mmmhmm! I need you to come out to the forest with me. Something big's gonna happen. I can feel it! I need you to be there so you can see it to write it down. Mmmhmm!"

I could feel the energy burning through the receiver. He was on fire. "Yeah?" I asked.

"Yeah! Mmmhmm! C'mon. Get your shit on and get dressed! I'm coming to pick you up in ten minutes! Five minutes!"

"*Now?*"

"Yeah, now! C'mon! There's no time to waste. I have to go get Eleanor in Newport and we need to get there before midnight!"

"Or you'll turn into a pumpkin?" I asked.

"C'mon! C'mon! Are you in or out? I need you, man! Let's go!"

I looked over at my wife and she was nestling back into her sleep. There wasn't a peep coming from my daughter's room; it had the feel like she might make it through the night without waking up. I looked over at the clock at it read *10:42*. I was in my underwear. I could easily tell him to get lost and climb into bed. But it was the eve of the millennium and I hadn't even gone out. I just felt like I should do *something*, and the whiskey was prodding me towards adventure. This could be perfect in the eyes of my wife. It wasn't like I was going out partying or anything, but I still got to get out and do something half-crazy.

I looked down at my glass and over at the half-full pint sitting on the counter. "You're driving?" I asked.

"I'm driving," he said.

"Then I'm in."

The next thing I knew we were walking through the woods, just the three of us. It was Matt, Eleanor and I. I looked down and watched Eleanor's boots skidding awkwardly along the crusty, frozen snow. They belonged to one of Matt's sons and were a little too big for her. Her white pearl-colored heels were back in the truck, resting on a pile of old newspapers, work-gloves and hard hats. That image just about said it all, right there. Imagine the odds of this rich, powerful woman leaving perhaps one of the most exclusive parties in the world to come ride in a pickup truck and walk through the woods. That was a trip—pulling up to the Rosecliff Mansion in Matt's dented little Dodge pickup, amidst the Bentleys and Mercedes that lined the parking circle, and scooping up a wool-clad socialite from the entrance.

Though it didn't seem to phase Eleanor. She was different. She wore a long black wool coat over her evening gown. She wore no hat. Her nose and her ears were pink from the chill and her whitish hair had come unfurled in the soft winter wind. Matt was dressed like he dressed for work, like he always dressed, in his lined navy chaps, maroon fleece jacket and his black NK Sailing skull cap tugged down to his eyebrows. I was dressed like I was ready to go skiing. I had my old white shell with the coffee stains on it (a little something I like to call *The White Delight*) and my black waterproof snow pants on, and was even wearing and old pair of telemark ski boots that were impenetrable by water. I had the pint inside my jacket pocket. I unscrewed the cap, took a sip, and winced.

"You want to borrow my hat, Eleanor?" I asked.

She looked over at me and smiled. "No. Thank you, Shamus," she said.

"Let me know if you change your mind. I'm fine. You can have some of this whiskey, too, if you want. It'll warm you right up."

"Thank you," she said, not looking at me this time. "I'm fine."

It was a cold and clear night under a three-quarter moon. The moonlight played off the snow and lit up the forest around it. The only sounds came from the soft breeze blowing through the air and our feet crunching along the old crusty snow. It was a truly beautiful night. We were walking through the meadow on the way to the forest. Under the moonlight you could see all the way across to the far side of the field, with the moon shining brighter in one streak near the center of the field and the tall grasses casting a shadow over the bluish snow.

I thought about how nice it was, just being out there, and then realized how quiet Matt was being. I never had time to think like this around him.

"What are you so quiet for?" I asked him, my voice cutting through the night and sounding twice as loud as I expected.

"I feel like I'm not supposed to talk," he said quietly. "Shut up," he said and smiled. "Just be quiet and observe… you drunk," he added.

"Gladly," I said.

We walked through the remainder of the meadow without saying a word to one another. Our feet crunched and crunched until we came to the stream that led into the forest. Matt held his arm out so Eleanor could steady herself in her oversized boots as she crossed the wooden planks to the other side. I followed them over.

I felt the change again as we moved away from the river and under the canopy of the first big beeches of the forest. And this time, it was more profound than ever before. It was like I was stepping into a vacuum. I felt the pressure change and the frequency of the night dropped an octave in my eardrums. There was no longer any wind. All was completely still and silent. The moonlight filtered in through the canopy and the low outstretched limbs, casting odd shadows everywhere. The entire forest was a contrast of white, cutting beams of moonlight and dark shadows.

We all stood still together on the outskirts of the forest.

"Do you feel that?" Matt asked.

I nodded.

"It's beautiful," Eleanor said.

"Mmmhmm," Matt said, almost whispering. "I *knew* it." He looked down at his old digital wristwatch. "11:53," he said. "C'mon. We need to get to the mother beech before midnight."

Matt started off along the trail and we followed. I pulled up the rear of the pack, behind Eleanor. Matt was focused on his goal and walking quickly and Eleanor couldn't quite keep up in her sloppy boots, so we dragged behind a bit. I heard the sounds of our feet crunching through the snow; mine hard and plodding and Eleanor's dragging and scraping, like she was cross-country skiing along the surface. Gradually, and almost imperceptibly at first, I began to notice another sound building around us. It was a soft hum in between the scraping and plodding of our boots. Eleanor stopped in front of me so I stopped, too. I looked ahead and Matt had also stopped. I listened. It was the softest of hums, but it was definitely there. It was almost like the sound you hear when there's complete silence and all there is, is an odd frequency ringing in your eardrums. Only it was different. There was a different tone to it. It had an almost musical quality. I wondered if it was just me who was hearing it; if it was from the whiskey or maybe from playing music with the amplifier turned up too loud. But if it was just me, then why were Matt and Eleanor standing still as well?

"Oh!" Eleanor remarked in a breathy whisper.

Matt was standing about twenty feet ahead of us on the path, smiling and waving his arm for us to come forward. "C'mon!" he said, whispering. "It's okay. This is *good*!"

Matt started up again and we followed him along the path. The sound seemed to disappear when we resumed walking, but after I got used to the sound of our feet again, it came back. And it was getting stronger and stronger as we walked until I could hear it clearly and constantly over the top of our footsteps. It was getting stronger as we got closer to the heart of the forest.

"Holy shit," I whispered to myself.

"Don't say that!" Eleanor scolded. "Don't curse. Don't even talk, please."

"All right," I said. "I'm sorry. I didn't even know I was doing it… it just came out."

"*Shush!*" she said.

Ordinarily I would have been a bit upset by being *shushed* by anyone except my mom, but this time I didn't even think about it. As we walked along I looked at the forest all around me. It was crazy, alive. The contrast between shadow and darkness was constantly shifting. The shadows were changing shape and dancing. I paused for a moment to see if it was just my movement that was making them dance. I couldn't be sure. Maybe it was the wind up high in the branches. Maybe it was something else. The humming got louder.

Eleanor broke into an awkward run, dragging her boots along the surface of the snow and straining her stiff joints to their full extent in an effort to catch up to Matt. I walked faster, then eventually broke into a light jog to keep pace. I was giggling as I ran, beside myself in fascination. I found it odd that I wasn't scared at all. I felt completely safe and happy.

Matt was standing underneath the canopy of the old mother beech, grinning, waiting for us. "Can you guys hear that, or is it just me?" he asked.

"No, we hear it," Eleanor said.

I nodded.

"It's so beautiful," she whispered.

We stood and listened. It *was* beautiful. It never changed in pitch but I thought of it as a song nonetheless. It was a hundred of the same notes wrapped around each other in a high hum that wavered in intensity but never faltered.

"Here," Matt said. "This is what you gotta do."

He strode over to the mother beech tree, flung his arms out wide, and fell into in with a big bear hug. He wrapped his arms around it tight, with his fingertips stretching just beyond the halfway mark around the trunk. He pressed his cheek against the bark and nuzzled into it. "You gotta give it a hug," he said.

There was an explosion overhead that lit up the night sky to the south. It startled me at first until it was followed by others like it in rapid succession. It was fireworks, popping and streaming red and yellow and green and trailing off into dust. It was First Night in downtown Newport, and the celebration was just beginning.

As the first few pops and bolts of light disrupted the silence, the forest came to life. The bushes rustled around the outskirts of the forest and the birds came pouring out of them. They soared out and flew low underneath the canopy and directly at us, and came to light in the tip-top branches of the mother beech. There must have been hundreds of them, and every one of them was calling out their squawking song, talking to each other.

I looked over at Eleanor and she was crying. There were tears streaming down her cheeks and she was smiling. Matt stepped away from the tree to comfort her and she rushed past him and embraced the tree. And she stood there in her tailored wool jacket, her pearls and her ball gown, weeping, caressing the tree underneath an exploding sky.

CHAPTER 23

Thirteen days later, in the early evening while Matt was in his basement office researching the latest ivory-billed woodpecker developments, the phone rang. It was Eleanor.

"Matthew," she said, breathlessly. Her voice sounded strained, almost in panic.

"Eleanor? Oh, hey! Hi! What's the matter? It sounds like something's the matter."

"No," she said. "We did it! We did it, Matthew! The forest is saved!"

Matt stood there in his thermal underwear, frozen.

"Are... are you there?" she asked.

"Yeah," Matt said, and it sounded to him like he was listening to himself say it from inside his body.

"Did you hear me? I said the forest is saved!"

"Yeah," he said again, distantly. A smile began to creep over his face. "I mean... it's unbelievable. Mmmhmm! Mmmhmm! Mmmhmmm!"

"Can you believe it?" she asked. "We did it!"

"I know! I know! But... how? I mean... what happened?" Matt asked.

"I told you, Matthew. It's all about the money. We received a huge, last-minute donation from a source who wishes to remain anonymous. It's... miraculous! We contacted the developers again with the new offer and they couldn't refuse. They're turning a profit on the land, now. That's all they care about."

"Wow!" Matt exclaimed. He yanked at the sliver-gray tufts of hair over his ears. "Anonymous? They don't even want credit for it?"

"The money was wired to me along with a note. It was very generous... it accounts for nearly forty percent of our offer."

"And they said 'yes'?"

"Of course! They had to! To not take it at this point would be... near suicide for the corporation. They'd be vilified by the press. Absolutely destroyed! Matthew... I'm sorry but I have to go. I have so many people to call and thank and tell them the news. But I wanted to call you first. You were very important in all of this. Sincerely, we couldn't have done it without you."

Matt shook his head. "We couldn't have done it without *you*. *You're* the one who did everything."

"You're too modest," she said. "This is just the beginning for you. You're the voice of the forest, remember?"

Matt smiled. "I *am*, aren't I? The Twig!"

"That's right," she said, laughing. "We'll be holding a dedication ceremony in the early Spring as soon as the snow melts. Everyone will be there; the Land Trust, the

Nature Conservancy, The Watershed Association, and the developers, of course. We're giving them some good press for selling to us... making it seem like their charity has somehow played a role in this. And it has, in a way. They *could* have still refused and taken their chances with the negative publicity."

"Yeah! Mmmhmm! Are the news crews going to be there?"

"Absolutely. We'll have them interview you again! You're the face of the operation."

"The operation!" Matt repeated, bemused.

"That's right. After the dedication we'll all walk the woods with trash bags and clean-up any litter that's around. Maybe you and your crew could clean out some of the unsightly downed branches around the walking trails."

"Sure!"

"Thank you, Matthew. I'll talk to you soon," she said, and hung up.

Matt hung up the phone and stood and stared at it. His heart was racing. He began pacing the hallway in his basement, grinning, stomping hard on the floor and massaging the gray tufts of hair over his ears.

❧

Nine hours later Matt was in his basement, bleary-eyed, pacing the halls in the dark and tearing at the gray tufts of hair over his ears. Always it came back to this. First there was the round of phone calls to everyone he knew that had even remotely expressed an interest in the forest. That ended at about eleven when it became obvious that he was waking people up and no one was in the mood. Then there was more pacing. He tried laying down in bed several times and found his eyes pried open and his heart pumping loud and hard in his chest. In between there was pacing, mindless tv watching, and more pacing.

Now it was four-thirty in the morning. He could hear his heart thudding away in there with the house so quiet around him. There was no use. His mouth was dry and his hands were trembling. It was fight or flight and there was nobody to fight, so he had to get the hell out of there. Where to go? There seemed only one logical place; the forest.

Matt looked out the window into the blue black night and thought he saw traces of snow. He flipped on the porch light to watch the first few flakes of the storm drift down lazily to the ground. He went upstairs to make some coffee and get dressed.

❧

It was a near whiteout on the roads on the way to the forest. Matt blasted through the storm in his little black pickup. The wind was howling and the snow was absurd. He was the only one out on the roads. When he got up to the crest of the Newport bridge he was assaulted by a heavy gust of wind and involuntarily skipped over the double yellow lines on the slick road. At that point, he thought briefly about turning back. But there was no way to turn around on the bridge and this would surely be the worst of it. Matt slowed down and leaned way over the steering wheel, desperately searching for the road through his burning eyes. "Mmmhmm! Mmmhmm," he repeated at sporadic intervals to calm himself.

By the time he got into Portsmouth the plows had joined him out on the roads. It was still dark but the skies had lightened a shade behind the wall of white. He turned off into the development that abutted the forest. The street was unplowed. His tires spun and grabbed, spun and grabbed, jerking him down the road. He had four-wheel drive but his tires were ridiculously bald. He scolded himself for it. Why did he always have to wait until things were completely broken to get them fixed? Damn it! He wasn't sure if he could make it.

The back side of the forest was only a few hundred feet ahead. This wasn't the side with the long meadow and the formal entrance, but if he hiked through a few backyards he could get there. Matt pulled over on the side of the road. He left his truck there with the hazard lights flashing and started walking.

It was beautiful out there. The wind was blowing gentler now and the snow was falling nearly straight down. It was silent except for the sounds of the plows scraping away off in the distance. Matt plodded through backyards with his eye on the forest. The trees were taking on more dimension as the black night sky became bluer with the coming daylight. The sun was preparing to burst forth over the horizon. Matt looked into the windows of the houses he passed to see if anyone was watching him. The windows were all dark. He thought he heard a voice calling to him and stopped to listen.

There was nothing except the near silence of the snow falling.

He resumed walking and thought he heard it again, so he stopped to listen.

"Matt," sounded a faint voice from behind him, back towards the road.

Matt whipped around. "Who is that? Is somebody there?"

"Matt! Matt!" called the voice, this time seemingly from the direction of the forest.

Matt turned and started running toward the forest, with his loosely tied muck boots flopping around underneath him. It sounded like the guys on his crew. What the hell were they doing out here?

"Timmy? Shame?" he called out, stepping over a broken stone wall and tromping into the outskirts of the forest. He was short of breath so he stopped to listen again.

This time there was nothing. His breath shot out in warm steamy bursts and the forest was calm all around him. It was wet, winter wonderland snow that piled up on the fat horizontal limbs of the beeches low to the ground. The snow was starting to pile up and was about to cover the few patches of brown leaf litter that remained. The trees swayed slightly in the breeze and creaked.

How could that be? He *knew* he heard someone calling him. He heard the plow getting closer out on the road, so he ran back towards it. It seemed farther than he remembered on the way back. His lungs were burning and his legs were heavy. At last, he stumbled out onto the road just before the plow got to his truck and waved down the plow guy.

The guy was in a big ten-wheeler with a sander on the back. He unrolled the window and looked at Matt strangely. He had a dark scruffy face and the look of a man who'd been through all kinds of storms in his life. "You all right?" he asked.

Matt gasped for breath. "Is there anybody else out here?" he asked.

The guy hesitated. "Out where?"

"I don't know," Matt said, frustrated. "Out on the road or out in the woods."

"Out in the woods?"

"Anywhere. Is there anyone else out here?"

The guy shrugged. "I don't know. There's another guy in a plow on the other side of the neighborhood. Are you all right, man? You need some help or something?"

"No," Matt answered firmly. "I just thought I heard someone calling me, that's all. Forget it."

"All right," the guy said, unconvinced but anxious to get back to work. "Hey—can you move your truck for me? I don't want to plow you in."

"Oh! Mmmhmmm! Yeah! Sure!" Matt boomed.

He got back in his truck and pulled a three-point turn to head back out to the main road. The back end of his truck fishtailed and pulled and jerked along the fresh snow. He was still thinking about the voices. It was so strange. There *had* to be someone else out there. Someone who knew him. Unless he was losing it from sleep deprivation. Maybe he was shot from being so anxious all night. That had to take a lot out of the nervous system. It was like the day after an acid trip, he recalled. Sometimes that was even more bizarre than the trip itself.

He pulled out onto the main road just in time to see the truck coming at him. It was an eighteen-wheeler jack-knifed, sliding sideways down the wrong side of the street, coming right at him.

This is it? Matt thought. *It's going to end on the best day of my life? The day of the best thing that ever happened to me in my life is also going to be the day of the unluckiest? It's so funny, that way.*

The truck was sliding noiselessly in slow motion directly at his windshield. It was getting larger and more real. Death was imminent. Matt closed his eyes and was okay with it.

He tensed up and waited for the impact, and waited... and waited. He heard the sound of air-brakes unlocking and the gargling of a big engine. He opened his eyes to find the rear end of the tractor-trailer parked six inches from his front bumper. On the rear bumper of the trailer was a green bumper sticker with white lettering that read, "TREES ARE COOL."

CHAPTER 24

Everyone was there for the big day.

Matt was there with the whole family behind him; his two twelve year-old twin boys Pete and Gary, and his wife Kay. Matt called her "Cowgirl Kay." He'd stolen her away from a small Texas town and brought her up north with him forever. She was Texas tough. Kay wasn't exactly actively supportive of Matt's preservation mission. It didn't mean as much to her. She kind of supported him by keeping her distance and letting him do his own thing when it came to the tree stuff. But today she was proud and smiling in the sun with her big oval sunglasses and wavy red-brown hair. She was happy.

It was hard not to be, with the sun shining and the new green buds nearly ready to pop on the trees, and so much having been accomplished. We were out in the parking area at the trailhead where the meadow began for the dedication ceremony. It was April and the sun was warm enough to be out there without a jacket. It was mud season, and the ground was soft and mushy underneath our feet.

The posts of the newly installed trail map and information signs were surrounded by oozing mud. The small crowd stood gathered close to the trailhead, surrounding a small PA system and a microphone.

Courtney and Vivian and I were there for the show. I held onto Viv, with my arms hooked under her thighs and her body nuzzled close to my chest. We were standing with Tim and Weeman (who had made a point of telling Matt right before the ceremony that he was still a loser and just got lucky this time.)

Eleanor was there, happier than I'd ever seen her. She looked like she could fly away if she felt like it. She was standing with a bunch of contributors and people from the Land Trust and Watershed Association, who were all feeling about just as good as she was.

The news crews were there, with their trucks set up back in the parking area and their cameras focused on the microphone.

Jim Trent was addressing the crowd, surrounded by his development cronies with big plastic smiles on their faces. Jim squinted into the sun through his thick-rimmed glasses and gave a heartwarming speech about the importance of corporate responsibility. He explained how sometimes when things of true importance are involved, like our environment, it was necessary to set aside big business and accept responsibility. Sometimes you had to do what was right, he said. He explained how happy they were to be able to preserve this area so that future generations could enjoy it and benefit from it just as our ancestors did. It was a heartwarming speech indeed, unless you knew that he only did it because he got paid, which nearly everyone present did. But Mr. Trent did it with true aplomb. I'm sure it made a great impression on the tv audience.

Matt was set to speak next, and it was Trent's job to introduce him. He made no mention of accusations or restraining orders, but rather told the audience that Matt had been "instrumental in achieving our goals of preserving this great stand of wilderness." As he walked away from the microphone and Matt went towards it, they were forced to cross paths. Matt gave him a big grin, looked him right in the eye and went for the old two-hand handshake. Trent returned it and smiled for the cameras, but never once looked at Matt or said a word to him. He broke it off as quickly as was socially acceptable and returned to the side of his cronies.

Matt bumped into the microphone, causing it to squeak and putter, and got a nice round of applause from the crowd. There were people whistling and Tim, Weeman and I were yelling, "Mickey! Mickey!"

Matt had his thumbs hooked in the straps of his bib overall chaps, grinning as he spoke. "Yeah! Mmmhmm! This is awesome!" he began. He paused for a moment and let the applause die down. His grin slowly faded and his face took on a slight scowl. He suddenly felt a wide range of emotions all at once. He couldn't understand what he was feeling, and it annoyed him. "I don't know what I should say," he began. "That's never happened to me before. Anyone who knows me, they know. Talking usually isn't a problem for me. It's just... this place is so special and it's such a great victory for the earth to still have it... it's hard to pick the right words."

There were tears coming from his eyes. He wiped them away, swallowed hard, and pulled out some index cards from his pocket. "I brought some notes with me, filled up with some old clichés that I thought seemed really relevant... but I'm not going to read them. Words aren't really good enough for what we did here. I'm just going to talk from the heart. I just want to thank everyone who made a donation to help save this place, and especially Eleanor Higgins for all her hard work."

Here the crowd gave a nice round of applause for Eleanor, who blushed under the attention.

"I guess what I just wanted to say is... look at me," Matt continued, holding his arms out to the sides. "I'm just a tree guy. I'm not that smart and I'm not any kind of scientist or anything, but look what I've accomplished—with a lot of help, obviously, but still. I'm living proof that anyone can make a difference when it comes to our environment. You just have to care about it enough, and be willing to do something about it. It *is* the little things that matter. Any little thing that you can do counts for something. And then a whole bunch of little things add up and you get something like this."

The crowd applauded him again.

"Yeah!" he said, and chuckled. "Well... let's get out and enjoy it! Grab those trash bags and let's go!"

❧

There was very little trash out there in the forest. It was more for the symbolic gesture of it that we were doing it,

I think. Everyone was having a good time, just walking around under the trees and enjoying the weather.

Matt's sons, Pete and Gary, were little mop-headed wild-men. They were running around all over the place, whacking each other in the shins with sticks. I was watching them go at it, remembering the way my little brother and I used to do the same type of stuff. Usually the game ended when one of us got mad or got hurt. It didn't take long. They were pouncing around off the trail and one of them twisted his ankle on something and went down in a heap.

I saw it coming, so I was first on the scene. I handed the baby over to Court and jogged over there to help him out. I think it was Pete who was down, but I couldn't be sure because they looked so much alike. One of them needed a haircut, or a birthmark on his face or something.

"You all right little buddy?" I asked him, offering my hand to help him up.

"Ahh!" he winced, holding his ankle and rocking back and forth, trying to be tough. "I fell on something buried there, I think," he said, pointing a few feet behind him to a spot where the leaf-litter was mounded up slightly from the rest of the ground.

"Probably a stump or something," I said.

I went back to inspect it and kicked at the mound with the heel of my boot, expecting some resistance from a stump or stone underneath. Instead, the earth gave way and what appeared to be a small statue rolled out from under it. The texture was odd; it was like it was stone but it was porous and light. I'd never seen anything like it before. I bent over it and began to feel a chill when I saw that it had small wings sticking out of its shoulders. The chill got greater as I wiped the muck away to see the face of an angel with eyes raised to the heavens and a halo wrapped around its hair. I stayed there, bent over, looking at it but not believing it.

"What is it?" asked Pete, (or Gary for that matter.)

I turned around and showed him.

"It's an angel," he said. And then louder, snatching it from me and holding it up over his head like a trophy, "It's an angel! Hey, dad! Look at this!"

The other boy was down on his knees about twenty feet away, wiping the muck away from another one. This one was plastic and painted, with rosy pink cheeks, golden hair and a blue dress.

I looked around and saw there were small rises in the leaf-litter all around us. Soon everyone was surrounding us, hunting through the leaves in search of a prize. Eleanor was down on her hands and knees in her spring dress, wiping the muck away from another one. There were angels coming up all over the place. Some were big and some were small, some were broken and some were whole, some were stone and others were plastic or ceramic, but they were all angels. There must have been twenty-five or thirty of them buried in there.

I looked over and Matt was standing close by off to my left, in between the trunks of two big beech trees.

He looked at me and his eyes were saucers reflecting electric light. "Crystal," he said, hoarsely.

I nodded. "I think I'll write it, now," I told him.

EPILOGUE

Presidential Seal
The White House
Washington

December 18, 1999

Personal

Mr. Matthew Largess
Rhode Island Tree Council
1995 Smith Street
North Providence, RI 02911

Dear Matthew,

I enjoyed my visit to Newport very much and was delighted with the warm welcome I received.

Thank you for the copy of *Voice of the Forest* and the calendar. I appreciate your thoughtfulness and generosity, and Hillary joins me in sending best wishes.

Sincerely,
Bill Clinton

ABOUT THE AUTHOR

Shamus Flaherty graduated from the University of New Hampshire in 1998 with a BA in English Literature. He has written three novels: *The Great Blowout* (Authorhouse 2002), *Blue Collar Heaven* (Authorhouse 2005), and *Treehugger* (Authorhouse 2009).

Flaherty lives in Jamestown, RI with his wife and two daughters. Besides writing he enjoys beers, landscaping, family time, music and long walks on the beach. He is the lead guitarist, singer and songwriter for the revolutionary rock band The Real Makers.

For more information on books and music by Shamus Flaherty, visit www.realmakersband.com

Manufactured By: RR Donnelley
Breinigsville, PA USA
January, 2011